In Each Moment

An African-American Anthology of Short Stories About Life & Love

Written by:
Michelle Rhnea Yisrael

Published by I AM Media Books

ISBN: 978-1-951667-16-0
Published by I AM Media Books, Michigan, USA
Media to Awaken the World!

www.iammediabooks.com

Table of Contents

1

In Need of Comfort

She suddenly felt uneasy. She passed the corner store and saw a tall slender man wearing a white turban. She guessed he was only a few years older than her Uncle Ray. She'd seen him before with the men dressed in white who preached...no screamed, at people on 87th Street at the Dan Ryan where she got on the train to go to Columbia College. Regularly, they stood on the corner screaming at people and asked if they knew who they were. They held Bibles in their hands, but she rarely saw them open and read from them and when they did, they shouted a bunch of reviling. Chasah wondered if the Bible's main function was to make people feel damned. She'd overheard her grandfather and uncles arguing about that same thing at every family gathering for the last two years. Uncle Ray never took the time anymore to talk to her about life and share the family stories, like he used to.

Uncle Ray was the first one to start the Bible argument and he wouldn't let up. He seemed to have an agenda and his agenda was to bring discord in this family. To her it seemed as though he came to the family gatherings just to pretend to be better than everybody else, because he now thought differently about his life. She heard her grandfather say Uncle Ray was being "righteous over much." Chasah Googled it. It came from the book of Ecclesiastes 7:16, "Be not righteous overmuch; neither make thyself over wise: why shouldest thou destroy thyself?" As she reflected upon the verse, she thought it meant for someone to be self-righteous and judgmental; thinking they are better or more righteous than others. Or being so righteous they forget to enjoy life, love the people around them, and be a good example of virtue and honor.

Chasah even heard Uncle Ray announce that he wouldn't eat the BBQ ribs anymore.

"That swine!" He'd call it.

So, whenever it was time to eat, Auntie Christa fixed him a plate of greens, potato salad, macaroni and cheese and chicken. He would never say chicken was *"that swine."* Chasah noticed he put the plate Auntie Christa gave him on any table and never came back to eat it. He was offensive and pushed his family away with his contentiousness. He even got mad if anyone called him Uncle Ray. He wanted everyone to call him Zebulun. Everybody seemed perplexed when he came to this new way of thinking and expected his entire family to walk in his shoes; nobody understood why. Their lack of understanding frustrated him and kept him in a constant state of anger. He didn't seem to have patience enough to get his point across. If causing your family to resent your presence was typical of this new way of thinking, Chasah decided she wanted no part of it. Ever!

This same man she saw at the corner store also passed her most evenings under the viaduct walking from the bus stop. She guessed he was coming from work since she never saw him carrying books. Her uncles warned her to be careful walking under that viaduct.

"You're a beauty Chasah," they warned. *"Many men won't know how to handle you. You will have to sift through the junk to get you a decent young man who will cherish and protect you. Don't you settle."*

Chasah was a true beauty to behold. She was well-formed with a striking hourglass figure; the essence of The Commodores' *"Brickhouse"*, turning the heads of men young and old as she strutted down the street unconscious of her own natural sensuality. It was a natural walk—she didn't have to practice. Each time she walked past a male with wanton eyes, she stiffened and awkwardly tried desperately to change the way she walked.

"She moves like a Maltese kitten," a security guard once whispered in the campus hallway.

They didn't know whether to watch her buttocks or her thick, rounded, sexy calves as she sauntered. She didn't walk, she sashayed. Her uncles said Chasah's mother moved the same way, before she aged and gained weight. She was well-balanced and agile. She had a stealthy stride, which made her buttocks twitch methodically, ever so gently, from one side to another with an innate simplicity. Her dresses were never too short, and it was evident she was taught to wear a slip under her dresses, unlike most young women these days. She made a conscious effort not to wear her dresses to short or her pants too tight. At any rate, watching her sensual stroll brought life to many a man on the street corner.

One year and six months after Chasah and Jake met during math class, things took a turn. He transferred to Columbia from Tuskegee in the fall term and they were in the same group in that math class. They enrolled in the statistics course together the last day of the fall semester, just before winter break. As she remembered it, they were supposed to meet up after her last literature class and go to Jake's house to spend time together. They hadn't seen each other, except in statistics class or study group, in more than two weeks. When they talked the night before, they were both excited about being on break for almost three weeks and looked forward to the possibility of spending time together.

She waited outside the theater until a security guard kept trying to talk to her. He made her uncomfortable with his advances. Chasah felt as though she needed protection from pushy men all the time. She waited outside at the front door until there were only five people remaining at the busy bus stop on the corner. *Could he have walked right past her?* She stood there so long she began to feel ashamed for waiting.

Finally, she decided to get on the next bus. She swiped her bus pass and attempted to walk down the aisle with a heavy bag on her shoulder. Jake would have helped with her bag. Suddenly, she felt a sneeze attack her in the middle of an attempt to pull the handicap seat down. The driver pulled off and she lost her balance. She grabbed the only thing she could to keep from falling, a man's arm. He stiffened, making his body strong and stable enough for her to get her bearings as she struggled to sit down. She had no apprehension in grabbing his arm and he didn't pull back. He had her back; he was her railing. As she settled into the seat, she thanked him. He simply nodded his head.

Her thoughts raced back to Jake. She wanted to get home so she could be there when he called.

"I knew I should have went back home to get my cell phone this morning," she whispered to herself.

Instead, Chasah chose to catch her train and get to class on time. She knew Jake was probably blowing up her phone by now. She didn't know how she missed him; she stood in the same spot she'd stood many times while she waited for him. He always came. She didn't need her cell phone before to catch up to him. There had been times when her phone was still in her bag and on silent, yet he found her. It never took this long. So, she was anxious to hear his explanation for standing her up.

Chasah waited for Jake's phone call for seven days. She dialed his number four times that week. The first time, there was no answer. The second time, no answer. Again, the third time. The fourth time she called, she got a busy signal. She fought with herself about dialing his cell again, she didn't like how it felt to be so clingy and possessive. She wondered if he was locked up, so she asked his friend Cory and he said he hadn't seen Jake either. It was common for young men to disappear for a time in the hood. Her mother would always get so angry when she drove around the city and saw the police demanding young brothers stretch their arms on the top of the car while being searched. Many times, it was for no apparent reason. Her own brother was stopped because of his locs all the time.

Jake told her not to come to his house unless he was expecting her, because his younger brother always had his friends over, who were known gangbangers. Jake's father was killed in the county jail when they were younger; and their mother was always at work. Chasah walked over there anyway, it was only a few blocks away. She did see his mother's car when she walked up, so she decided to ring the bell. His brother and friends were on the porch smoking blunts, even though it was cold outside. They heckled her as she approached the porch and wouldn't let her up the stairs.

Jake's brother quipped, *"What do you want? My brother ain't here."*

"Can I ring the bell to talk to your mom?" she begged.

"For what? I said he ain't here, you ain't gone be bothering my mama", his brother snapped angrily.

"I just wanted to ask her a question," Chasah responded.

"You ain't gone be asking my mama no questions. If Jake wanted to talk to you, he would have called you. Did you call his phone?" he taunted.

"Yes, but he's not answering," she responded sheepishly.

"Then I ain't got nothin to tell you either!" he said as he appeared to bark at her. *"If my brother wanted to talk to you girl, he would have called you."*

Chasah turned around confused and hurt.

Someone in their math study group picked up a flyer in the library about an event promoted by Sunshine Moxie Entertainment at the Exstacy Lounge on North Avenue and Dearborn. King

Corso was opening the pre-party show for Bigbellyrelli to celebrate the end of the semester, and Chasah wanted to make sure she was there. Everybody said they were going. They all bought tickets, including Jake. She had been in the house all week, since it was winter and cold outside. She had no place to go so she stayed inside and spent the week in her room reading. She thought Jake would be at the party too. She hoped he would. It was very unlike him to not call her. They usually talked on the phone for hours every evening, sometimes talking about nothing, sometimes talking about everything. Sometimes just holding up the line. Neither wanted to let the other go.

Chasah planned a therapeutic bath, because she thought it would calm the churning in her stomach, which disconcerted her thoughts since the last day of the semester. She deliberately soaked in the tub in preparation for the party. When the water cooled, she added more hot water. When the bubbles subsided, she added more bubble bath. She needed ambiance, so she turned off the lights and lit a Hawaiian scented candle. She washed every part of her body. Taking a long, hot bath comforted and made her feel good.

After her bath, she put powder and perfume on everywhere she could think of. She wanted to smell good. A long, relaxing bath and taking time to spruce herself up was an enjoyable practice she'd learn to neglect later in her life. She chose to wear a svelte red dress her auntie bought her as a birthday gift. She oiled, brushed, and curled her hair so it would sit on her head just so. She prided herself in her very large and well-kept natural hair. She loved her natural hair. She decided to wear a twist out because Jake liked it that way. She felt special because God made Black hair so strong and beautiful. She wondered why the Muslim girl she passed in the halls every Thursday kept her beautiful hair covered all the time. She didn't think God made their beautiful black hair to be tied up all the time. Like her sensuous walk, Chasah's natural hair turned many heads.

Chasah left home for the party feeling confident she looked and smelled good enough for someone to eat. She was certain Jake would be at the party, since the organizers were both their friends. She was ready to talk to Jake with the confidence of an innocent fawn grazing in the woods, unaware of the wolf approaching his prey at a snail's pace. She practiced what she'd say to Jake in the mirror. She couldn't wait to see his smiling face and give her ear to hear his reasons for standing her up and altering their carefully constructed plans.

Chasah and Jake liked Bigbellyrelli and King Corso. Bigbellyrelli gave his audience a nice balance between jazz, R & B and hip hop. He was her favorite. But it was really difficult to enjoy the show without Jake. Chasah danced until she was ready to drop. She danced with or without a partner. It didn't matter, she simply enjoyed dancing. She danced until her feet and legs felt numb. She loved to dance even that day, the disappointment of Jake not being there didn't stop her. She paid little attention to the latest dance craze. She just moved every part of her body to the music. She was always in sync. Music had always been in her bones. She should have learned to play an instrument. Music was soothing and relaxing to her. That night she didn't slow dance, she saved that for Jake.

Chasah wanted to get as close to Jake as she could. She wanted to lean on him, supported by his strong body and his big arms. She wanted to be comforted by both his touch and the music simultaneously. The anticipation of his touch made her dance even more. She kept her eyes on the door, waiting for Jake to enter. The party was nearly over before she realized, he was not coming. They were supposed to go to that party together. She went alone and he never showed. She wondered if he remembered. She wanted to talk to him, he had been her best friend since they first met a year and a half ago. She wanted to look into his kind eyes. Little did she know, she'd learn to live with that achy feeling, the pain of yearning for Jake. It was a pain she'd learn to hate and at the same time look forward to with anticipation.

Chasah just turned 19. She should never have gone to that party alone on public transportation. She was on her way home at midnight, alone. She should have called an Uber. To get from the bus stop to her house, she needed to walk about five blocks, pass under a long viaduct, and walk across a series of vacant lots. She usually walked that walk faster looking around her cautiously. She was usually conscious of every noise and jumped at every sound. That evening, she was distracted. She wasn't paying close attention to her surroundings. She was both exhausted from her night of excited dancing and somber, because she hadn't seen nor heard from Jake in a week. She kept her arms bundled tight, because of Chicago's winter chill.

As she approached the end of the viaduct on the way home, she heard footsteps behind her. The streets were deserted because of the cold and time of night. She turned her head slightly, to try to see who was walking behind her without breaking her own stride. She walked faster. He picked up his stride. She thought of running, but her feet were numb, and she had a difficult time picking them up quickly. Before she knew it, the footsteps caught up with her. Abruptly, there was an arm around her neck. A smelly skull cap was slid over her head covering her face. The perpetrator then put a knife to her throat. It seemed as if he did it all at the same time, in one smooth and swift swoop. It seemed as if he had much skill and practice. She wondered how many other young girls were preyed on by him. There was no delay in the steps he took to secure Chasah as his prey.

He whispered in a fierce tone, *"Do what I tell you and you won't get killed. Scream or try to run, and I'll stick this knife in your neck."*

Chasah was petrified. She didn't make a sound. He pulled her over to the stairs where passengers came down from the Metra train. There was not a sole in eyesight or earshot, from what she could tell

"No!" whimpered Chasah

"Shut up!" he retorted. *"This is what happens to the daughters of Zion who are haughty and walk with stretched forth necks and wanton eyes. I see you walking and mincing as you go and*

making a tinkling with your feet. You don't cover yourself. What did you think was going to happen? You asked for it. Well, I'm giving it to you."

Her attacker timed it perfectly. While he performed his fiendish act, no train stopped at the station. She listened for a train. She paid close attention to his voice trying to remember it. He put his hand over her mouth, as his hips bounced up and down on her torso like an animal and pushed her back into the edge of the steps causing her more pain. Chasah knew Jake, as it was biblically coined. He had loved her tenderly for six months. He didn't enter her with such rough force. This was different, the assailant's poisonous rod invaded her hidden place hatefully. Tears rolled down her face, and she whimpered from the abuse.

"Shut up, you better dry up those tears, I ain't hurtin you, you ain't tight. You done this before, more than once. You're a bad girl!" he said gritting his teeth.

He moved the knife closer to her throat as he spoke. Chasah was afraid not to do what she was told and managed to suck up her tears.

"Move your hips damn it, you know how to do this!" Chasah moved her hips slowly as he humped.

"Damn you, move faster. I am almost there!" he snarled.
Chasah could feel the tip of the knife penetrate the skin in her neck. She recognized his voice, but she wasn't sure where she'd heard it.

"Please don't hurt me," cried Chasah. *"Please stop."* she wept.

"Kiss my neck," he moaned. She delicately rubbed her nose and checks on his neck and moved it around being careful not to let it touch her lips.

"Please stop!" sniveled Chasah.

"Shut up! Take it out and put it in my mouth," ordered the perpetrator as he gently jabbed at her breasts with the tip of his knife.

Chasah submitted unenthusiastically, took a deep breath and wept quietly.

"Bad girl, I told you to shut up and do what I tell you to do!" screeched the attacker. *"No! Don't*

try to use both hands," he corrected her as he stuck tip of his knife closer to her neck again. He pushed harder to pin one arm under her. He lifted the skull cap up just slightly under her nose.

"Open your mouth and kiss me now!" he groaned. *"I can make you feel good. You know you want it. I seen you walk,"* he murmured. *"I been watching you."*

"No, please!" Chasah sobbed.

"Don't let me tell you to shut up one more time. I told you to kiss me," he grumbled his final order before she heard his last deep groan and his venom spewed in her hidden place. He tightened his squeeze on her for what seemed like forever. Chasah felt her own hidden place pulsate and cascade as he squeezed her.

"Bad girl," he whispered.

Chasah's heart lamented low and deep, she was betrayed by her own body. She felt a deep shame. Indeed, she was a *bad girl.* She sighed.

Her attacker finished and got up quickly, *"Don't take that hat off your head until I tell you to."*

He ran off in the same direction from which he came. Chasah thought she heard his footsteps moving toward the gate. She laid there for a bit, until she couldn't feel his presence around her anymore. She was afraid get up, afraid to look after him. She got up after a few more minutes, pulled the skull cap off her face, looked around her slowly and deliberately, and then ran home, despite the numbness in her feet and legs.

She tried to close her coat as she ran but noticed the buttons had been ripped off. Everything happened so fast, she didn't notice when he ripped her coat open. She didn't want anyone to find her torn panties and underwear, so she picked them up and stuffed them in her pocket. She had on one shoe and could not find the other.

It wasn't until she hurled herself into the door that she could feel the sting of his heavy brutal hand across her face, her bruised and throbbing lady parts, and the reminiscent aching from his fist in her stomach. Her mother jumped out of bed. She was finally able to scream loudly, enough to startle everyone in the house. Words finally poured out of her mouth. As Chasah told her mother what happened, she held her and rocked her. Her mother rarely hugged her.

Chasah felt safe and secure at home in her mother's embrace.

When the police came, they asked so many questions. According to them, she did everything wrong. She wondered how they would have reacted had it been them in her place. Their tone was accusatory. When she was taken to the hospital, she was examined. The doctor said the tear in her lady parts wasn't bad enough for stitches. Once the doctor discovered Chasah wasn't a virgin, he became as suspicious as the officers.

Chasah felt awful. She felt dirty. She felt it was her own fault. She couldn't identify her rapist, because she did not even try to get a look at him. Their voices were accusatory. They couldn't understand she did not want to see his face. She just wanted him to leave her alone. She just wanted the police and the doctor to leave her alone now as well. She didn't like their tone and the way they treated her. She didn't even like the way they questioned her mother in an interrogatory manner. Her father came to the hospital. He and her mother had not lived together since Chasah as a little girl. Her mother always called him when there was an emergency, and he always came.

No one knew, except her immediate family, that Chasah was violated because of the sensual

22

stroll that came to her from the one who made her. No one could ever know how her lady parts betrayed her, which would be her secret forever. Unlike the memory of her Jake, this memory was like a poignant wound in the heart. Her youthful naiveté was stolen, vanished forever after her rape.

That voice though, she wanted to remember. She listened for the fierce voice almost every day. For a long time, she wondered what would have happened if she had screamed or tried to run away. Maybe she could have gotten away. She remembered being frozen. Maybe her screams would have been heard by someone. She didn't know why she made it so easy for her rapist, that's what the police told her. She was just scared, too scared to do anything other than follow instructions. She felt sick and guilty when the police officer asked her several times why she didn't scream or at least try to run. She wondered why too. The thought of a knife stuck in her throat wouldn't allow her to do anything but what she did. She was powerless against his weapon, was her conclusion.

The voice she heard was not the voice of a teenager. It was not the arms of a little boy. He didn't feel like a largely built man, but he was a man just the same. Nobody except her mother and her uncle said she did the right thing. They both told her maybe had she not cooperated, she may not even be alive to tell her story and feel the comfort of the words they spoke to her.

She could still feel the bitter cold as she lay there under the brutal attack. She could still feel the aching of a broken and naïve heart stolen. Chasah was haunted by the fact she did as she was told. Unable to hold back her tears, she followed every order. She was petrified and feared her attacker would slit her throat. She did not know what else to do. She was sorry she even went to that party. She was even more sorry she went alone. It was the last time Chasah walked that walk alone. Five blocks. In the dark. From the bus stop. Under the viaduct. Past the series of vacant lots to where she lived.

Chasah remembers his voice even today. Several years later she heard that voice at the laundromat, as she pulled her head out of the dryer taking the clothes out. She didn't turn around. She made a beeline for the door, leaving all her family's laundry behind. She thought of nothing but getting out of there. Again, he had the advantage. She could recognize his voice, but she had no idea how he looked. Even now, as she ran out the door of the laundromat, she was afraid to look.

Chasah ran home and told her mother and uncle why she left the clothes at the laundry mat.

The two of them moved fast! They didn't seem
upset. Her mother picked up the phone
immediately and called the police. Her uncle
took Chasah's hand and walked to the door,
down the stairs, down the four blocks to the
laundromat. When they got there, there was
only a young woman and her children there
washing clothes. The police took a long time to
come. There was no sign of Chasah's attacker,
just more questions, another useless police
report, but thankfully no hospital and no probing
like the day of the attack.

During the violation, her rapist pulled at her
fine dress so roughly he tore the ruffle. He
ripped her panties off and raped her with what
seemed like all the force he could muster up.
His forceful entrance tore her vagina wall. It felt
as if he ripped the delicate layer of skin inside
her to pieces. Chasah remembers being afraid
and hurt. She remembers the tears. She
remembers his threats and how he said she better
act like she liked it. She remembers that horrific
night very well.

She could still hear his voice say, *"Make me
believe you, or I'll cut your throat."*

He also demanded that she rotate her hips, or
the knife would make its way to her chest. She

did as she was told. She did everything he commanded. She held her breath and touched her lips with his. She was careful not to let her tongue touch his tongue or his lips. She held it back hoping he wouldn't notice or care. She wanted to scream as she moved her hips in a circular motion. The scream was stuck in her chest. She couldn't pull it up for fear he'd make good on his threats.

Chasah stayed home for the rest of winter break. She didn't leave the house for any reason, except school for months after. Her uncle walked her to the bus stop every morning and he met her for the walk home in the afternoon. He stood there strongly each day when she got off that bus. Chasah loved her uncle, he acted like the father she didn't have. She was afraid to go out alone and he knew it. Chasah missed Jake, but those feelings were overshadowed by her fear of going out alone. She checked his Twitter Page. No activity. Snapchat. No activity. Instagram. No activity.

Chasah did not see Jake at school after winter break. She asked a few people if they'd seen him, they said no. Chasah could not understand what happened. She sent him a text. *"Message undeliverable."* She was so lonely and afraid, still. She felt so distraught from the attack. This made her open and vulnerable. She tried to go to his Facebook page and leave another message, but his page had disappeared.

Chasah saw the new transfer student, Gideon, in the cafeteria. They made eye contact. His stare was immediately intense, but it didn't unnerve her. He sat at the table in front of her with a friend. She could hardly focus on eating her lunch for watching him. As soon as their eyes met, she felt anger, instead of worry, for Jake. *Where was he and how could he disappear without one word?* She missed him. The last time she called his cell, she got a recording saying the number was disconnected. She used her break to read ahead for her next class. Gideon walked over to where she was and sat next to her. She was intrigued by the way he greeted her.

"Shalom Lil Princess."

"What does that mean? Does that mean the same as A salaam alaikum?"

"My name is Gideon."

Gideon began to explain his greeting and his name. She liked the way he explained things. He was gentle. He wasn't Jake, but his voice comforted her. Chasah admired his boldness.

27

Being shy and a bit of an introvert, it was easy to talk back to him. All she could do was answer his questions. She liked his name. Gideon. It was typical for her to shudder away and clamor up when approached by new people. She noticed she didn't stutter with Gideon though. He made her smile when he asked, *"Do you think you and I have a chance together?"*

She didn't know how to respond to his question since there was no break-up with Jake. In each moment, she listened and responded. She evaluated her reactions and attempted to come up with some sort of a catchy and hip phrase to say but couldn't and it didn't seem to matter to Gideon. She felt her face smiling and she felt the memory of Jake slowly slip to the back of her mind. She wanted to respond with something catchy or hip something memorable that he would think about later. She was a little excited, but uncertain.

She was nervous but felt a little bit of the loneliness leave her. She needed comfort and Gideon would do just fine. He seemed different from the other men her age around her. She felt like he could protect her. She felt safe, she never felt this safe with Jake. Gideon reminded her of how kind-hearted her Uncle Ray used to be. It was like she was being covered by a tented sanctuary; she didn't feel like a possession.

She felt freedom and safety when Gideon asked,
"Can I walk with you to your next class?"

2

At the End of the Day

Kayla loved to hear her daughter Keila and her oldest son Kaleb sing old school music. Kayla's love for R&B, especially blues, was passed on to her children. However, Keila still seemed to view the world and rhythm to the sounds of hip hop and rap music. Kayla hated it, but she tolerated it in the house for the sake of her daughter Keila and the other children feeling comfortable at home. She did not want them to feel like they had to steal away to their friend's homes, where parents were more lenient. Kayla did not mind Keila sitting in the living room playing her CD's. She knew Keila would be careful.

Kayla purchased a calendar a few years ago. Each month had an image of a different praise dancer. The calendar was adorned with images of praise dancers giving glory, honor and praise to the Heavenly Father through the ministry of dance and music. At the end of that year, she cut out the images, framed them, and hung the 12 lovely images throughout her apartment. They reminded her to keep her head in the right place.

A thought came to her mind as she looked at the praise dancers on her wall.

"I don't think I have ever felt this good in my life," she spoke loudly.

As she laid her clothes out for the next day, she thought about the difficulties she had trying to earn a college degree and raising her children alone. Then, according to her bitter aunt, she had the audacity to enroll in classes for business and marketing. She wanted to use her passion for crafting to open her own business. She thought it would be smart to study business and marketing first to help ensure her business' success.

It takes most people four years to finish a simple BA. It took Kayla eight years to finish because of her responsibilities of caring for her children. In each moment, she relished the time she spent with her children. Though she had the academic skills, she wanted to properly take care of her babies, because they meant a lot to her. She was not going to let life make her bitter.

It takes time to nurture and rear children properly. Kayla was proud of herself. She finally did it; they were all almost out of high school and adults! She wanted to encourage other single mothers to have enough courage, patience and pride within themselves and to pass it to their daughters and sons. Kayla didn't think about being alone as much as she used to. She spent her time just trying to get through each day. She was free to love, yet nobody was in her life who wanted to love her. She was fine with that. She learned that one does not have to be lonely when they are alone. In each moment, she contemplated the joys of freedom; she knew it was going to be another lovely day the Lord made, and she was getting better at rejoicing when faced with another day.

Growing up in Chicago and battling the harsh winters, Kayla loved the lakefront beaches, the parks, and the zoo. She loved spending her time listening to the percussionists engage in their regular jam sessions at the 63rd Street beach. She was afraid to get out there herself with her Shakore', so she used her fingers to tap out the beats on her steering wheel. Kayla also liked to read while she sat there or watch the families have such a great time barbecuing and picnicking outside the beach area. There was always something free to do on the lakefront in Chicago, especially in the summer. In the winter, there was always something to do throughout the city.

Kayla liked the line dance classes in Dolton on Thursday nights. She still loved to dance.

Being the place where stepping was created, Kayla could always find a steppers class to attend that didn't cost too much. This way, she was entertained and got in a good workout at the same time. Dancing kept her looking good. The museums were fantastic, and they still had one free day each week for visitors like Kayla. Even though gang violence was taking over some areas of the city, Chicago was a marvelous place and she loved living there. She didn't mind doing anything alone anymore. Besides it was much better than being someone's temp or side piece. Besides, Kayla was waiting to be found by her Boaz.

It was finally getting warm and the sun shone longer, giving her more daylight to walk on the lake. Kayla rushed out of the house to pick up the boys from school and take them to baseball practice. She'd arranged for her sister to pick up Keila and take her to the *Daughters of Sarah* class at the Knesset. She felt accomplished to have been able to be consistent with keeping herself and the children active in the Knesset for so long. She was hoping one of the brothers would try and date her, but she guessed they were afraid of a sister with three children.

She had time to stop at the same Walgreens where she always stopped. She wanted to pick up some Emergen-C packets before the boys finished. She parked her car at the back of the parking lot as she always did to ensure she increased the number of steps she took every day. It was easy to reach her goal of 10,000 steps every day and it was not uncommon for her Apple watch to report 15,000 steps when she made time to take those walks on the lake.

As Kayla got out of the car, put her earphones in her ear and walked across the parking lot, she was almost run into by a dark colored van. She held her phone case tightly in her hand, as it was important. It held her whole life. Her credit card was in it, work ID, driver's license, insurance card and all the stuff she needed, instead of a large cumbersome purse. The same homeless gentlemen she saw last time as she entered the store stood there again asking people to use the ATM inside.

"Can you go to the ATM and get some money out, and help me?"

Whatever happened to people asking for a lil change? The last time she gave him $1. That's all she had. She didn't usually have cash or coins on hand. He asked her for a dollar.

"I don't have one," Kayla snapped. She wasn't even to the door yet.

"How about when you come out!"

Kayla kept walking. She walked deliberately down the aisle to get to where she knew she'd find the Emergen-C packs. The store didn't seem so crowded on the way in, and she got through the check out pretty quickly. *"Early evening is a good time to go to Walgreens,"* she thought as she swiped her card to check out. Her main thoughts though were to get to the park before baseball practice ended. She didn't like them waiting outside for her. She wanted to be there as they came out of the door. She wanted her boys to be safe and she feared children being alone unsupervised in the park, especially so close to sundown. She had to then get to the Knesset to pick up Keila before her *Daughters of Sarah* class ended. *"Darn!"* remembering she wanted to get that quick walk on the lake in also. That might not happen this evening.

When Kayla walked out of the store the homeless man said, *"Can I get a dollar now?"*

Kayla was suddenly pissed. She quickly and quietly responded, *"For one, they don't give dollars."* She felt insulted. *"Didn't you just get a check on the first?"*

"That was three days ago," eased out of his mouth so easily.

"HELL NO!" Thought Kayla. Instead, she retorted, *"You didn't give ME none of that!"*

With gall, the beggar said, *"You didn't ask."*

Kayla was too through and she sped up her walk to the car across the parking lot. She noticed her right shoestring was loose but would wait to tie it when she got her boys in the car. One stop was enough. She noticed the same dark van approaching ahead of her and to her right, so she walked closer to the parked cars on her left. One thing she didn't want to happen was to get ran over by some no driving, indecisive driver. The van slowed down and seemed come too close as it seemed to pass her. Kayla slowed down to let the van pass, her aim was to pick up her babies on time.

The parking lot was just about empty. The van came to an abrupt stop. The side door was snatched open and a white man with dark hair and a black hoodie jumped out of the van, grabbed her in an almost bear hug, and threw her in the van, before jumping in himself and slamming it shut. Kayla screamed in astonishment as she was snatched. She dropped

her bag, keys and phone case. The police arrived
after being called by an older woman sitting in
her car. She'd seen everything.

"It happened so fast!" she screamed.

The police found her right shoe where Kayla was
accosted in plain view of the security camera.

3

Under a Dark Shadow

The first time Aliyah heard him, she stood in the bathroom listening through their shared wall for ten minutes and debated over what would happen if she called the landlord to report the disturbance. Living in this large building was very different from living in the duplex over a senior citizen couple, Abah Hosea and Emah Adeevah, and their two cats in the South Suburbs. She really missed the place. She felt safe there. They treated her like a daughter and called her baht. She was sad Abah Hosea passed away so suddenly. She was perplexed when their son came from LA to put his own mother in a nursing home and sell her home out from under her.

Aliyah tried to tell Robert she would care for his mother, but he wasn't having it. He obviously didn't want to take care of his own mother, yet he wouldn't allow her to do it, and she wanted to. Aliyah thought of Emah Adeevah as the grandmother she never had. She loved the attention Emah gave her daughter Naomi. Aliyah thought it would be a better idea for Robert to take his mother back to California with him. He wouldn't think of that either.

As Aliyah listened to the voice coming from the other side of the bathroom wall, she felt a tingle in her legs. After a few minutes, she wasn't disturbed any longer but intrigued. He was always so loud, but he had a really good voice. Unlike hers, it was made for singing. During the five weeks she'd lived in the building, she never heard a female voice coming from behind the other side of the wall.

"Is he married? Or does he have a lady friend? He sounds like he could be a little older, not much, but maybe a little? What does he do for a living? Is he a singer for real? If he is, then why doesn't he sing any original songs? So, he must not be a real singer? Then what does he do? Why don't I ever see?"

Aliyah was not disturbed anymore. Instead she had questions. She'd decided the next time she heard his key in the door next to hers, then she'd make up a reason to go out into the hallway.

"What does he look like?" she thought out loud.

She left the bathroom because she felt like an intruder listening to her next-door neighbor in his bathroom.

"OOO, this ain't right," she murmured. Before turning to leave though she decided to knock on the wall.

"Sh, sh, sh", she uttered loudly as she knocked.

She was startled by the sudden silence. Then he began to sing again. This time though, she could tell he tried to lower his voice.

"Well at least he is thoughtful," she said to herself as she left the bathroom to go into her bedroom.

Teaching at South Suburban Community College Early College was Aliyah Dauid's first assignment. She chose her outfit carefully. It was a pink and gray business suit she got from Ashley Stuarts' clearance rack. She wanted to get her feet securely in the door and get past the 90-day probationary period before breaking out in full garb.

As she looked at herself in the mirror, she asked herself, *"Who the hell are you?"*

Aliyah knew she needed to be more conscious of what she ate, and she needed to work out. She hated her size. She didn't remember when she gained the extra pounds, but she had a difficult time finding an outfit that fit and would give her the professional look she sought. She wanted to make a good first impression on her colleagues as well as her students. She was eager and very nervous about this position.

Initially, Aliyah wanted to teach eighth grade at a middle school. She wasn't sure if she could handle the maturity of today's high school students. However, after being overlooked for the perfect position twice, she felt she better take this job. It would give her the experience she needed to re-apply for the position she really wanted. She spent the entire evening before preparing for her debut as an English teacher. She wanted to make sure she got her bluff in right away with these students.

SSC Early College was known to be a little rough. She reviewed several issues of The T.R.U.S.T. Restorative Classroom Management manual taking note of common occurrences she might face tomorrow. If she could survive at an alternative high school for at-risk youth, she could survive anywhere. She carefully chose a reading assignment that might be of interest to the students. It was a short story about a family struggling to make it and overcoming many trials and tribulations. She wanted to encourage her students to have courage, patience, and pride within themselves. Aliyah decided to have her students read the story she chose and write about how much strength and pride the family in the story needed to make it through their day.

She let her daughter Naomi read the story for approval. She was ten years old going on forty. Naomi was very mature for her age, because she was an avid reader. She was glad her daughter was not born a boy. She feared a boy would genetically hold Benjamin's darkness. She felt like she could better influence a daughter to be good inside by being her example.

Naomi missed her Abah. Before they left, Aliyah made sure she wrote Benjamin a long letter explaining he could see Naomi anytime he wanted. She told him she preferred to drop Naomi off at Softah's house whenever they wanted to see her. He was to call her sister Linda to make visiting arrangements. Aliyah thought it through thoroughly. She also went to his Emah's house and let her know the plan too. She never told Softah where she lived, so Softah would not have to lie to her son.

Aliyah loved Benjamin's Emah; she was always kind to her. How could Aliyah make Emah understand, Benjamin made her fear for her life? Before she left, Aliyah explained to his mom her plan and why she felt she had to go.

Emah smiled at her and said, *"I know sweetheart, I was married to Benjamin's daddy, remember."* Then she gave Aliyah a long tight squeeze. *"You are a brave young woman, be happy. Just don't forget your God."*

Softah had been asking for Naomi one weekend a month for the past six months when she got her social security check. Naomi enjoyed being at Softah's house baking and working in her garden. Softah loved for Naomi to read to her at night. Benjamin never came to see Naomi while she was at Softa's house, and he never left a message for a special visit either.

When Benjamin wanted to support Naomi financially, he could deposit money into an account with Naomi's name on it at the Chase Bank right down the street from him or leave it with Softah. Aliyah tried to make it easy, but she was not going to beg; or take him to court for child support. She was going to let that be between him and Yah. In the meantime, she got on her knees everyday asking Yah to provide for her baby since her daddy would not.

It was common to find both Aliyah and Naomi curled up on the chaise lounge together in their new place reading. They read silently as well as out loud to each other. Like Aliyah, Naomi has always been academic levels above the rest of her class. There was a bookshelf in every room, including the bathroom and kitchen. Aliyah was a mother who spent much time with her little girl. She became interested in teaching as she volunteered at Naomi's school and helped her with her homework. Just before Naomi's sixth birthday, Aliyah organized a play group, which met once per week at her apartment.

Aliyah felt safe living in the high rise in Hyde Park, because they had tight security, and no one could get on the elevator unless they were expected. The security guard always checked. She never discussed any of this with Naomi; she was very careful not to talk badly to her daughter about her dad. She was trying to do the right thing. She simply wanted peace and love, of course.

Aliyah loved to hear Naomi sing old school music. It was a kind of family legacy. The music of the late sixties 60's to mid-70's, where lyrics

43

were less important than rhythm and actual musical instruments. Aliyah's father was a master drummer and he caused her to appreciate good music. Now, Aliyah wanted her daughter Naomi to learn to appreciate pure music just like her father taught her to love it.

"Emah, can I get an IPOD when you get your first paycheck?" asked Naomi.

"Let's talk about it after the third or fourth paycheck," Aliyah said. *"The rent is paid for only one more month, I ain't buying no extra stuff for a while,"* she said to herself.

Aliyah loved art and decor that depicted her heritage. Her house was filled with pictures of mothers and their children, praise dancers who seemed to be having a good time, as well as men working and taking care of business. She purchased a piece from an auction that was simply a giant West African baobab tree standing strong and firm near a body of water, as she knew her people to be. There was a mountain and waterfall behind it. The tree reminded her of the nobility and the strength of those first "migrants" stolen from the shores of their homeland and shipped to a land of criminal strangers. This piece gave Aliyah a feeling of peace and serenity. She hung it on the wall at the foot of her bed.

As she laid her clothes out on the sofa, she thought about the difficulties she had trying to finish high school and raise a child alone. Then, she found the courage to enroll in college. Her own mother told her she needed to go get a job. It takes most people four years to finish college. It took Aliyah six. She wanted a different life, a better one, a life with more quality. That takes time. She was proud of herself. She finally did it! She was much better than Popeye's Chicken.

"Oooo, that's my song!" She stopped her reflective moment to dance. *"Ooh-ooh-oh-ooh-oh-ooh-Ooh-ooh-oh-ooh-Ooh, yeah, baby. Whoa-whoa-oh-oh-Mmm..."*

Aliyah allowed her body to get wrapped up in the music. In each moment, she listened, she snapped her fingers and let her arms and feet be moved by the rhythm behind the words.
"It's so nice to have a man around to lend a helping hand, you can bet. Yeah!" mumbled Aliyah, as she danced to the Temptations.

This song was not necessarily an old skool jam, but shoot, Aliyah thought. *"Cause I believe a woman should be treated with the utmost respect, mmm-hmmm..."* she danced and sang along.

"Whoa whoa, oh oh, mmm..., I need a man to touch me," she added.

Aliyah wasn't sure whether she missed Benjamin because she yearned to be touched or

45

because she really desired his company. She hadn't let herself think about him in a while and she wouldn't now either. He didn't deserve her thoughts.

"Now I like openin' doors, Pickin' up Yeah, her hanky Yeah off the floor. Treat her like a lady..." she sang along.

The song made her feel like she missed out on being treated well. She was not a feminist, and women's lib was not her thing, so the words to the song caused her to want a man to open doors for her and block the traffic keeping her safe as she crossed the street. It made her long for the compliments from a man such as the lyrics described. As she listened to the tempting Temptations sing to her, she thought about the couple who lived next door. He treated his wife this way. Aliyah never experienced that type of treatment, yet she longed for it. She was happy for her neighbors.

"Who's gonna touch me?" Aliyah lamented softly to herself. She didn't want Naomi to hear her.

The music gave her something to look forward to. It made her feel the possibilities and the hope of love. She did not want to forget that. The music gave her hope. She closed her eyes, bobbed her head, and let the music permeate her.

"Man, that's my song, one day someone is going to love me," she muttered again as a tear made its way down her cheek. She sat down in her favorite chair and just snapped her fingers and bobbed her head and moaned, *"Man, sometimes it hurts."* She said too loudly.

"What did you say Emah?" shouted Naomi from her room.

"Nothin lil girl, just singing my song. You are playing Emah some good music this evening." Aliyah shouted back to her. She was a Temptations buff.

It was Benjamin's touch that held her hostage. She needed to stop toying with herself before she picked up the phone to call him to tell him where they'd moved. She missed being touched. Instead, she remembered the sickened pain she felt in the pit of her stomach the last time she saw him as he stood outside her car peering at her through his sunglasses as he told her that she was never in his corner, because she wouldn't skip her class to go with him to pick up his new business cards before the print shop closed.

"You want to wear the pants in this relationship. You probably gonna meet some other nigga."

Benjamin was a skilled teacher. In fact, that is what drew Aliyah to Benjamin in the first place. He knew his way around the Book. She was excited for him and proud he was teaching Bible class that night, she hoped it would change him. She hadn't been to Thursday night Bible class since the semester started. She didn't think it was an occasion to miss an important psychology class. He didn't like her choice.

"Why you can't believe I love you and I'm not trying to be with nobody else. I want to make this work with you," she begged. *"I'm glad you are teaching tonight and I believe you will do well, but I can't miss class tonight. I will go back after this semester is over,"* she promised.

She loved encouraging him, but he couldn't find it in his heart to share in her moments as well. He took submission too far. He accused her of not knowing how to submit, but he didn't know how to cause her to want to submit.

Suddenly, Aliyah remembered that Benjamin was the reason she was ostracized. He told one brother at Bible class she slept with some brother at the university and the lie spread like wildfire. At Sabbath fellowship, the brothers wouldn't allow their wives to talk to her. She looked Amirah in her face and greeted her with a warm happy *"Shalom"*, but Amirah gave her a stony face and did not return her greeting. When she took time and care to clean, fold, and deliver books, lightly used toys, and baby clothes to

48

Sister Eve, her husband, brother Jeremiah, returned them to Aliyah.

"My wife can't accept these from you," he stabbed.

Aliyah knew why these things were happening to her and she refused to defend herself to these people, these friends, who were supposed to be her family. The feast committee would not even accept her food she tried to contribute to the last feast. This was Benjamin's family; they were not hers. They proved that when they turned on her because of his lies. The effects of this horrible secret really devastated her when it spilled over into another part of their lives. Benjamin gas-lighted her whenever he did not want to take responsibility for his actions. He tried to make her think it was her fault; as if she did something to cause him to do it. He was skillful in this deceit and she was becoming as good at it as he was. Each time he promised this was the last time.

When Aliyah and Benjamin were alone one night, she asked him why he kept reneging on his promise to stop. Aliyah's heart dropped to her feet as she felt a tinge of blood fall to her cheek from the corner of her mouth. As she continued to feel the throbbing of his fists on her injured, now bruised face and on her battered chest as he straddled her, she could not twist her torso enough to get away from his fist in her stomach. She remembered all the times

49

Benjamin used his tongue to abuse her and fists to assault her over and over again. This time because she merely questioned him.

"A submissive wife will never question her head," he shouted. *"Why do you always make me punish you? If I don't punish you, The Most High will, and you won't like it. Believe me. It will not feel good. He will have your eternal soul."*

"I'm sorry Lord, please forgive me for questioning you," Aliyah shrieked loudly as she tried to twist her body from Benjamin's grips.

"Look at you, you are still not submissive, you refuse to take your punishment. Who is Lord of this house? Who is head? Who wears the pants?"

When Aliyah woke up, she was lying on the couch and Benjamin was kneeled over her telling her to wake up. Naomi was standing in the doorway watching and listening. *What were they teaching her? What example was she setting for her daughter?*

"You need to be more submissive and obey your lord. If you don't, I will get another wife to show you how it is done. No other brother in the fellowship has this problem with their wives. You are an embarrassment and I will take great pleasure in breaking your Jezebel spirit. You

50

cannot question me; I am your teacher and I am your lord!" he cried with literal tears.

In the 10 years they were together, Benjamin accused Aliyah of trying to wear the pants in the family and jeopardizing his lordship and reign many times, but it was never this ruthless. This was not just the usual back hand or smack in the face. On a few occasions, her punishment was a whooping with his leather belt as if she were a mischievous child. This battering was finally the catalyst for her to leave him. Emotional abuse has scars the world cannot see, but when coupled with physical abuse, it is a devastating and incapacitating knock-out punch combination. *How can a woman love a man who beats her?*

Finally, after years of living in terror, Aliyah mustered up enough strength and courage to remove herself and her child from the grips of the mean man and his lack of confidence. She learned a man who lacks confidence in himself and in God is a dangerous man, whom no woman can change. She was labeled a whore, a sinful woman, a liar, and an unruly female who wanted to lead her husband instead of allowing him to lead her. The whole "family" feared her.

Aliyah feared these same people who feared her, because she was afraid of how judgmental and unforgiving, she learned they could be. They didn't care to realize a good woman doesn't leave a good man without good cause. Benjamin was the kind of man who loved intensely, but more times than not, he was extremely incompetent as a benevolent husband.

Aliyah feared she'd be alone for the rest of her life. In each moment, she lived without the fellowship of the so-called "sisters and brothers" who abandoned her, she thought about living this life of fear and realized she was not afraid of death at all. Her greatest fear was being alone. Aliyah felt stupid for even thinking of picking up the phone. She didn't have to fight making that call anymore. She remembered why she walked away, and she felt sick and tired of being accused of not being in his corner when it was him who was not in her corner.

Aliyah was afraid of Benjamin's lies he spread through the "family" to cover his tracks, because he believed, with all his being, she was the cause. She feared things would get worse as his insecurities grew. The more she tried making their lives better, the worse he got.

"Stop it, don't be stupid. You know how it will end. Let him go. He doesn't need to know where we are", she reminded herself. Aliyah thanked Yah for the escape. As soon as she was settled in her new place and her new job, she would find someplace else to fellowship on the Sabbath. She missed fellowship, but she'd never stop living the lifestyle and she never stopped teaching it to her daughter and being her example.

"Naomi, it's almost time for bed. You can stop being the DJ now. Do you have your clothes and book bag ready for tomorrow? We don't want to get up with too many things to do in the morning.

I cannot be late for my first day," she shouted redirecting her own thoughts more than instructing the little DJ in the other room.

She was not going to let her thoughts take her back there, and she was not going to be distracted from making her first assignment a good experience for her students. *"Get a grip girl, keep the darkness at bay."*

As Aliyah put her baby girl to bed and listened to her nightly ritual of saying ten things for which her daughter was thankful, thoughts of the man who sang through her bathroom wall went in and out of her head until the next song on the playlist took over her thoughts completely. Aliyah began to be angry with herself for wanting to make that call. She was simply lonely and wanted to be touched.

"I need the comfort of a man," sang Stephanie Mills to Aliyah's lonely heart as she closed her eyes and imagined a man who was kind, loving, yet strong and protective. She dreamed of a man who was filled with The Fruit of the Spirit. She wanted him almost desperately. *"I need to change to gospel music to get my mind in a different place,"* as she switched to a different playlist. *"How about No Woman No Cry by Bob Marley,"* she said aloud. *"This may change my mood a bit.*

4

A Time to Love

Reuben didn't like being alone anymore. He couldn't remember when he wasn't alone. Though he worked two jobs and had people around him most of the time, his heart was in teaching. Reuben reflected on his work at the Los Angeles Community College, where he taught Criminal Justice. He thought about Richard, a young man in his Wednesday morning class.

Reuben had taught only a few young men like Richard in his four years as a college professor. He could see loneliness in the young man's eyes and suspected he was at his wit's end. Being a friend to loneliness, he knew it well. He invited Richard to join the spoken word group he chaperoned. He was playing psychologist and figured Richard would connect to the group, because of the brotherhood aura he created in the group. Reuben enjoyed mentoring young men and encouraging them to live in the hood, but not be of it.

He chose the proverbial black slacks to wear today. This time, he decided to go with a peach shirt and mildly colorful tie. His dress was usually very conservative. When Reuben left home that morning, he had a feeling it would be a special day.

Today he dressed in preparation for the blessing he knew he'd attract. After tying the tie snugly around his neck, he spotted the tweed jacket that went with his black pants. It was early spring, and mornings could be a bit nippy in the east wing of the college. Reuben wasn't new to the department chair position. His office was always chilly, and he wouldn't miss feeling that chill at all.

He was leaving in less than a week and Reuben felt melancholy about his West Coast days coming to an end. While preparing his usual breakfast of coffee, English muffins, and fresh melon salad, Reuben couldn't help but remember the reasons he was going back home to Chicago.

He'd be near his family, whom he missed, and he'd planned to make a real impact on the lives of young men in Chicago, who needed what he had to offer. Before going to his last meeting for department chairpersons, Reuben stopped by the registrar's office to submit his final grades. This was his last semester as Professor Reuben Dauid. He was moving to the Chicago Suburb of Homewood to start a new job as the principal of an alternative high school. He was anxious to be of service and sure the work would fulfil him. Plus, he'd be closer to his ailing father so he could help.

As Reuben entered the building of South Suburban Early College to start his new job his eyeballs caught sight of a fine sister in a pink and gray business suit, sauntering up the hallway towards him. He could sense she wasn't aware of the sensuality in her walk, she just walked. Her walk wasn't sexy, it was regal. She walked like a queen.

Reuben could sense her eagerness to teach. As he watched her walk into the office, he wondered if she would bring his blessing that day. *"She seemed to have chosen the outfit for her first day with care"*, Reuben thought. Her attire was stylish and had a flare of elegance, yet it was businesslike and professional. He spotted the pink that faintly appeared between the wool woven tightly together. The straight skirt accented her full figure. Yet the black wool made her stout curves appear slim.

Reuben loved a woman with a little meat on her bones. When he decided to choose a woman, he wanted one he could hold on to. He wanted one he could feel. He wanted to find out who this beautiful woman was. He imagined her warm smile seeming to invite him into her life. He wondered if she was already married or dating. Her ring finger was empty with no shadow. He wondered if she was soon to occupy at least some of his lonely time.

Reuben intentionally sped up his walk to catch up to her, so they'd get to the main office at the same time. He walked ahead to ensure he got to the office first. In each moment, he waited for her as he opened the door, held it in a gentlemanly manner so she could enter first, and greeted her with a kind and exhilarating smile, being careful not to be flirtatious as she walked in.

The smile he received in return was not standoffish, she was warm. Reuben could tell she held back deliberately, as she retained her regal air. In the back of his mind he felt he needed to be a better him, the expectation made his heart really flutter. His aim was to make this a special day as he contemplated the best way to make her smile. He knew it was time. He wanted to cause her to smile every day for the remainder of her life. In each moment, he thought about it, he remembered he was the new principal, he was the boss. *"I'm going to need a new job,"* he began to plan.

5

A Taste of Love

Yohanathan's Emah and Abah met in college, on the campus of Tuskegee University in the itty bitty city of Tuskegee, Alabama. His father was from the Southside of Chicago, and his mother was a native of Alabama ready to leave the first chance she got. She never understood why her family did not leave the south during The Great Migration. Her uncles left with the second wave in 1940. When her father came back from World War II, he decided to remain on the family land outside of Birmingham, Alabama and make the land work for him. Her father regretted his decision later, but was committed to the idea, so he stayed. Both her parents came from Black middle-class families with two parents in the home. In 1961, Yohanathan's mother and father entered the Tuskegee Institute graduating class together unbeknownst to one another until they met at Homecoming that year, when their love story began.

After they both graduated in 1961, they got married in 1962. Then, the newlyweds settled in Chicago, a few blocks from his mother's uncle and his family. The young couple started a real estate business. Their first purchase was a building on 47th in Bronzeville. The building had three small store fronts and four apartments above them. His father chose one store for his office and his mom opened a small Chicken and Waffles restaurant in another. She was a good cook and businesswoman. Both the businesses flourished. Yohanathan's parents rented the third storefront to a couple with whom they graduated, both Black doctors who serviced the segregated Southside community. They lived in one of the apartments and rented the others. It was a time when there were thriving businesses in the Black Chicago area and Yohanathan's parents were among them.

In 1968, after the death of Dr. Martin Luther King Jr., his parents attended a meeting of the Original Hebrew Israelite Nation on the city's South Side in search of self-identity and self-awareness. During those times, self was indicative to the Black community, rather than an individual person, very unlike today where the opposite exists. It was a time of Black unrest and White upheaval in the country. During Dr. King's fight against segregation in Chicago in 1966, Yohanathan's father said the mobs in Chicago were more hateful than the ones he'd experienced in Alabama and Mississippi. He described Chicago as a hateful and closed society. He set about helping the Blacks in Chicago open it up and Yohanathan's parents joined in the fight.

His parents joined the Chicago Freedom Movement when Yohanathan was just a boy. He remembered their fight against everything which helped to keep Chicago segregated: slumlords, realtors and Mayor Richard J. Daley's Democratic machine. It was a time when a revolution in black consciousness and an awakening was about to sweep the country. They found answers among the teachings of the Torah, as interpreted for them by two black "rabbis," Robert Divine and his assistant, Yehoshuah Sample. The teachers explained that the Black Hebrews were the direct descendants of the patriarchs, Abraham, Isaac and Jacob and the 10 lost tribes, who had been exiled from Israel for their sins and condemned to wander throughout Africa until they were kidnapped and sold into slavery in the Americas.

The day Dr. King was murdered, the school let the children out early. Yohanathan didn't know why until he got home. The teachers and principals cried as they dismissed the children. The walk home was quiet and dismal. The children knew something was wrong but did not know what until they reached their homes where parents were gathered around the television watching the news and getting angrier by the minute. Yohanathan witnessed rioting in the streets of Chicago, in his own neighborhood.

The assassination of Dr. King incited Black people to burn down businesses in their own communities. He saw the National Guard at the end of one corner and rioting looters at the other end. He witnessed a young White UPS driver ripped from his truck and beaten unmercifully by three young Black men. He saw looters carrying merchandise they hadn't purchased from the Woolworth's on the corner. He saw a Black barber standing outside his shop pleading with the rioters not to burn down his barber shop.

The year before, many families left the U.S. with Black Hebrew leader Ben Ami. After the riots, more families left, including Yohanathan's best friend James. Yohanathan's parents were tempted to leave the country as well. They chose to remain in Chicago instead. They made the decision to stay because in order to join the group they were required to sell their possessions, as Jesus directed the rich man, and turn the money over to the leaders of the group who would make travel arrangements and send a message regarding when it was time to leave. The money was also to be used for the sake of the group who mingled black history with the reading of the Old Testament.

The group adopted the ideas of Marcus Garvey, who led the Back-to-Africa movement in the 1920's. On an ultimate migration to the homeland of Israel, the leaders decided to direct people to settle in Liberia to purify the people first. Many never made it to Israel and those who did suffered hardship and came close to starvation first. The people who were able to return to Chicago, told stories of woe and adversity.

Yohanathan heard his parents say years later, after hearing about the hardships and sufferings of some people who left from personal friends who returned, that this was one of the best decisions they could have made for their family. The family never became members of a camp again, but they taught Yohanathan and his siblings how to live a lifestyle of righteousness. They closed their businesses every Saturday to observe the Sabbath and celebrated Holy Days. There were always a few families who joined them in the large backyard of their building for these celebrations.

Yohanathan remembers they never ate pork or shellfish again after they joined the Black Hebrew group. His mother even stopped serving it in her restaurant. Instead she served lamb chops, salmon, and red snapper. Yohanathan's favorite. They were committed to the new lifestyle and they taught their children to be committed to it as well. Yohanathan remembered very little of his pre-Black Hebrew life.

It was on the 4th day of The Feast of Tabernacles when Yohanathan looked up and watched his heart walk through the door of the restaurant. She was dressed in a midriff peach dress. The waist fit just tight enough to see she was a brick house and the bottom was wide enough for the air from the closing door to swish it lightly as if it were leaves on a tree. She wore it with a white lace wrap around her shoulders and a peach head wrap that looked as if it were wrapped for the queen of Ethiopia. He knew she would be his wife.

He graduated college the year prior and was to take over his father's real-estate business within a year upon his retirement. He had already made a few deals on his own so, his father knew the business would be in good hands. As Yohanathan watched her walk into the restaurant, he began to plan to love her and treat her with benevolence.

Six months later, Yohanathan tasted Ranya's mind and realized he had been starving for a gorgeous Israelite sister who could discuss The Word of God with intellect. They'd gotten to know each other well. They talked about everything. One day, while they talked about the reasons why Ruth and Boaz attracted each other's attention, he wanted nothing more than to sit with her under the stout swietenia humilis tree in the backyard of his winter home nestled in the beautiful mountains of Yalbac Hills in the Cayo district of Belize. Yohanathan loved his little haven in Central America. It was amazing that a young man of thirty-eight was able to earn enough money in real estate to purchase land in another country.

The striking swietenia humilis tree, which sprouts genuine mahogany wood, reminded him of the Baobab tree he saw sitting near the shores of the Bight of Benin in West Africa when he took his last trip. The tree was taller than a skyscraper in the city where he was born and at least as wide as half a football field. Yohanathan was a hopeless romantic, like his father and his grandfather. He was the third Yohanathan and he promised himself he'd teach his own sons to romance their wives as well. The tree in the backyard of his winter home was a symbol of his love for Ranya, which means song of God.

Yohanathan's mother taught him to respect women. His father taught him to never be ashamed to show kindness to his woman. Even when his parents argued, they were careful not to use hurtful words that they would later regret. There is no way to take those hurtful words back once they come out of your mouth. They practiced the skill of not letting the sun go down on wrath. He remembered them staying up many nights until they worked out their issues. And yet, you really didn't even know they were in the midst of an argument, because when their anger was heightened, they did not speak to one another above a whisper. Yohanathan learned they did this intentionally. It was one of the agreements of their marriage.

Yohanathan's father taught him to listen to his wife and to respect her opinion. He smiled each time he remembered his mother telling his father, when she thought he was making a mistake, *"You are not Ananias and I will not be your Sapphira."* His mother was like the sparklers' children play with on the fourth of July. Not a firecracker, which made a lot of noise with no splendor, but a sparkler, which brings both joy and splendor.

Yohanathan's father also taught him that marriage is a partnership, not a slave versus superior situation. He cleaned the kitchen after his wife cooked. When she was out late, whether working, visiting the sick, or at her women's group prayer meetings, he cooked dinner. He never treated his wife like she was a mere servant. While many men thought of their wives that way, Yohanathan never saw his father treat his mother as such. They were in that thing together and because he was a loving head of the household, their marriage lasted.

The formula he witnessed was that neither of them rarely thought about themselves. His father worked every day to make his wife smile and his mother worked every day to make his father smile. They submitted to one another. He never heard his mother complain about anything his father did, she talked to his father when she was not satisfied.

Alternately, he never heard his father complain to his buddies about his mother, he talked to her about his displeasure. They communicated openly, without fear of reprisal from the other. And they were a happy Black family, a light to the community.

In a time when Black men failed to provide because the system was set up to cause them to fail, Yohanathan's father never stopped trying. When business deals went south and grant monies failed to come through, his father knew that his mother would not look down on him and disrespect him when he failed at anything, and he didn't always succeed. While at the same time, she respected him when he tried. When he made a mistake or fell, he apologized to both God and his wife, then he got up and kept trying.

After they became part of the Black Hebrew community, Yohanathan saw his father pray and sometimes he would have Yohanathan pray right there beside him. He told his son that a righteous man may fall as he tries to be perfect in his daily walk, but what makes him righteous is that he gets back up. It was the trying which helped to keep their family strong. In each moment, Yohanathan reflected on his father's example of a benevolent husband, he wanted the same for his own life. Malachi 2:14 says: *"The Most High is witness to he and the wife of his youth."* Yohanathan knew Ranya could help him be a better man.

Yohanathan was ready for marriage. His only desire was to have the words which flowed from Ranya's tongue to his ears, be words of a virtuous and praying woman. She had that covered well. As they sat under that tree, he could feel his iron sharpening her iron, and her iron sharpening his iron as a result. She elevated his thinking to a level where he felt as if it were that moment and the twinkling of the eye he longed for.

He wanted to make love to her mind before he made love to her body. He savored every moment as they waited until the day of their marriage. They were both committed to no intercourse before they got their marriage license and both their blood and spiritual families could bear witness to their joyous occasion. Everything about Ranya made Yohanathan want to sing a song of praise to The Most High.

Wedding plans were underway when Yohanathan received news that Ranya and her bridesmaid were in a serious car accident. He ran to his car and raced to the hospital to be by his betrothed's bedside. When he got to the 4th floor intensive care unit, he saw Ranya's father holding his wife tightly as she wept into his chest. Her father looked up and locked eyes with Yohanathan and he immediately knew.

6

My Father's Sins

I am Meerah, the firstborn daughter of Israel's first king. The day my Abah, my daddy, King Saul, met Samuel was a glorious day for my family. Me, Emah, and my sister Michal danced and pranced and sang glory to God for our new station. That is, until we heard God's prophecy; the king would do wicked in the nation. Emah was a praying woman, you see. So, she told us to remember to always pray in order to save ourselves from God's condemnation.

My heart fell to the floor, and from that day to this, I watched my Abah fall. Because I was young, he wouldn't listen to me and being a mere woman didn't help none either. So, shoot, I just sat back and watched the sparks fly. If only he had prayed every day and kept all the Lord's commandments. If only he had submitted to that which was good in God's sight. It hurt me greatly to see my daddy make those five grave mistakes and fall away from God's light. When the Lord's spirit left my father, and a bad one overtook him, we immediately witnessed a terrible darkness like night.

First, after that big battle with the Philistines, he panicked. Instead of praying, asking God to help him by making all rough edges smooth and all crooked paths straight; he took matters into his own hands and went contrary to the law of sacrifice by making an offering himself. He needed for Samuel, the priest, to make that burnt offering, because it was the law and he knew it. Samuel was on his way, but my daddy wouldn't wait.

Next, in his haste and impatience he did something real stupid. He told the people to eat the meat they brought back as spoils of war. There is order in how we do things, but he proclaimed they do it without properly taking out all the blood first. He had the gall to proclaim it would not be a sin against the Lord. They may as well have eaten it raw. He had no right to put himself in God's place and change the law. I didn't eat because I was too afraid of what I saw.

Then, I knew all hell was gone break loose when he made his third mistake. When he led that big battle and slew those Amalekites. He was told to utterly destroy all they had and leave nothing to spare. But by then, my daddy King Saul was beside himself. I was shocked when he didn't follow the

Lord's instruction. When I saw the Amalekite King and his best sheep, oxen, and lamb being paraded down the center of the street, I fell to my knees and asked The Lord's mercy, because I knew my Abah was headed for sure destruction. My Abah should'na been greedy and tried to save the best for himself was my deduction. He left just too much room for Satan's vile induction.

Now I know my story is getting kinda long, so I'm gone try to wrap this up real quick. When I heard my father make excuses for saving that king and lie about trying to keep the best of the spoils for himself, my stomach became sick. You can't lie to God and not expect a swift kick. I didn't know no more what made my daddy tick.

My father's sins tore our family apart. He was suddenly blinded by jealousy for David, my brother Jonathan's best friend. My poor sister Michal wasn't praying every day like me and Emah. She made it easy for our father to use her as a pawn. She was given to David as a prized bride, but in a short while vehemently ripped away. She was traded to another. Michal couldn't be with the man who really adored her, is what I heard my Emah say.

It was all too much for me to see, he began to walk so bitterly. All I wanted my Abah to do was repent and fall to his knees. But that evil spirit wouldn't let him do it. And Emah? Oh, she really had a fit. In each moment, I watched; but all I could do was pray, watch and sit.

My Abah's sins almost destroyed Israel's entire nation. So much for my family's great station. But when Israel first kept pushing God for a king, He did foretell of that king's condemnation; which was my father's fall from salvation. My Abah's sins don't call for no adoration. He was destined to fall from the start. My father's sins greatly pierced my heart. His rise and fall tore our family apart. But as for me, "Heal me, O LORD, and I shall be healed; save me, and I shall be saved: for thou is my praise," I continued to pray and do my part.

7

Victimized By My Own Brothers

I am falling apart. I feel like my best days are
behind me. I can't shake it. I know I shamed my
family and my Emah keeps telling me it's my
fault. Why can't she see I'm hurt down deep in my
bones? They made me the victim. They did not
consider me at all. I am the sister of all brothers,
who don't try to grow in the Fruit of the Spirit.

Though only six of my brothers are born of my
mother, they all act the same. Leah, my mother, is
not like my grandmother, Sarah. She never speaks
up for me. She doesn't challenge my father or my
brothers with the truth about their behavior. They
get away with everything. She drives me crazy,
thinking she must be quietly agreeable all the time,
especially when wrongdoing runs rampant in our
family. These boys are out of control. I am not
going to disrespect her or anything but, these boys
take things too far. When I have children, I am
going to tell my sons when they are wrong.

Zilpah and Bilhah were a lot older than me, but
they were my friends. We would meet in Bilhah's
tent because Dodah Rachel gave her paint for her
lips and hair ornaments for her hair. She shared
them with me and Zilpah. I listened to them talk

and make plans for the happy life with the husbands of their dreams. They anticipated a husband would find them and pay their bondage price, marry them and sweep them off to some exotic land where they would bare his children. This all changed when Emah and Dodah used them as pawns in their war as part of an ongoing rivalry for my Abah's attention. I couldn't sneak in Bilhah's tent anymore and Zilpah had her own lion's share of problems to deal with. My family took away my friends. Is there no happiness for me?

There weren't many women in our little community. All I wanted were friends. In my naivety, I devised a plan. I made a basket of great chunky coils from water hyacinth stems and rope. Then I baked a loaf of bread and I picked berries and added it to the basket. I made cassia and peppermint oils noted as unmistakable fragrances and calming aromatic properties and added them to the basket. I wanted to show myself friendly, so I went out to visit the women of Shechem, where we'd made camp and where my Abah purchased the land where he had pitched his tent.

That's when I laid my eyes on Shechem. He was the prince of the land, and he was fine! I know I should have stopped him, but it was like love at first sight. I let him take me. I did not protest when he humbled me. Our souls were drawn to one another.

He said he loved me, and I believed him. He spoke so tenderly, and I wasn't promised to anyone, so in my mind what might happen could only be good. I wanted to be promised to him. We made a big mistake, but he tried really hard to make it right. Shechem asked Abah for my hand, to be his wife. He wanted me! Dinah. I was going to be the wife of the prince of the land. I was going to get away from my brothers and all their issues. I was anxious and I was excited too, but I was also so very scared our secret would be uncovered.

My brothers' behavior is an exploitative stench in my nose. You see, they wouldn't listen. And now…my lovely Shechem, his father Hamor and all the men of their city lay dead at the gate by the hands of my hotheaded brothers, Simeon and Levi. I tried to tell them and my other nine brothers that Shechem knew me, because I gave consent. Yes, what Shechem and I did was a violation of my familial boundaries, but I loved him.

We had cultural differences we were willing to overcome. He was following the culture of his own people, seeking fair trade and being neighborly. Shechem wasn't looking for love, neither was I. Didn't my word matter?

Shechem sought to hide me in his house, even his father tried to manipulate us out of what we thought was our secret. My brothers claim they were concerned with me being treated like a whore.

They were really more concerned with intermarriage among other nations than they were about my virtue. Why couldn't my brothers hear my voice? In their deceit, they thought they could control who people love.

Upon hearing the news, Abah was silent at first; then he tried to negotiate my marriage to Shechem. He knew there was no need to protect me, Shechem was tender, and he was not violent. To Abah, he appeared to be a man in love, not a man committing a violent act of rape. He could see I had no feelings of hostility and hatred toward Shechem, I didn't hate him. He looked in our eyes and felt the closeness and tenderness in both of us. So, he negotiated a reasonable truce and Shechem, his father, and all the men in their entourage were circumcised. Then, came the treachery.

My brothers deceived us all. They were treacherous and robbed me of a chance to marry my love and find security in a loving relationship. They were cruel, unjust and irrational. I feel as if someone punched me in my gut. They made us think if the men were all circumcised, then I would be given to Shechem for his wife. We had not a clue that the day they would be most sore during the healing, my crazy brothers would take their lives'.

When Abah found out that my brothers slaughtered innocent men in the night while they could not protect themselves, he seemed disgusted by their actions. Yet, his silence was reflective and cool spirited. His desire to act in a manner beneficial to both our family and the surrounding neighbors caused him to act quickly and critically to clean up my brother's disgraceful mess. And still, not one time, has anyone thought about me.

Now, my father Jacob has us packing our camels and running, again. Simeon and Levi's retaliation puts our family in jeopardy and makes peaceful coexistence impossible. Though Abah severely chided my brothers for their cowardice, he said we are headed for Bethel, the place of God, where he ran when Dod Esau chased him before any of us were born. He said we should always seek the God of his fathers' when we are in distress.

I still don't think he knows that my other Emah, or should I say my Dodah Rachel, is still hiding that strange idol she stole from Saba Laban's house when we fled. I saw her fondling it the night before; she didn't see me, but I saw her. Abah told us to leave all my Saba's idols where they were. Dodah Rachel had a hard time trusting in Abah's God, that was the difference between her and my Emah. Emah grew to believe in Him.

In each moment I breathe this story of love and violence. I need the women in my life to stop fighting and see I am grieving. I don't see why everyone is in distress. I am the one who was victimized. I'm the one who lost my love, I'll never be able to forget my Shechem and don't nobody care how I feel.

Abah rode alongside my camel for a while and talked to me about his God. He called Him Yah. Abah said Yah wanted to comfort me. He said Yah understood my pain and He knew my tears. I wanted to hug Abah for seeking me out to show empathy and compassion. I couldn't stop hurting. He said he wanted me to learn to seek his comfort from Yah.

"Walk with Yah like my Softah Sarah and my Emah Rebecca. Softah Sarah was faith filled and Emah Rebbecca was a sharp thinker. They were cunning, wailing women of prayer. They made Him their strength."

He told me how they walked with Yah, and in their walk with Him, they developed a lifestyle of praising Elohim. He said they made Yah their praise.

"They were intimate with Yah. The blessings they derived from such a close and intimate relationship with God brought healing, salvation and supernatural things into their lives. Angels spoke to Softah Sarah because of her intimacy with Yah."

Abah told me to just talk to Yah so I could learn to move a step further in my relationship with God every day. He explained that by making Him my praise, I would begin to see how Elohim would bring healing to my mind and body.

"He will also deliver you from the plans and attacks of the enemy because He is with you to heal and save you. Go through your day today knowing Yah is your praise," Abah explained while he comforted me.

"I've been so focused on my own problems I neglected to teach you to pray Dinah. I'm so sorry for my grave mistake. My word concerning their actions is that I refuse to accept any part of their vengeance. When we make camp at even, we can talk to Yah together, you have my word dear daughter."

I couldn't wait to get off that camel and hug him. After he smiled at me and told me he loved me, he left to check on the others.

"Next time, and there will be a next time, talk to me before making a decision about whom to give your affections," he whispered. *"Give me your word, daughter."*

"I give you my word Abah," I cried. My tears began to flow again, but this time, I began to talk to Yah as I cried. I needed His help. *"Heal me, O LORD, and I shall be healed; save me, and I shall be saved: for thou will become my praise,"* I prayed.

8

Healing Sprued Out

I

When it comes to you Lord, I'm limited
Here offering to you most willingly
tried to make peace with my brother as told
I'm grateful for having the mind to serve
Absolve me from hidden iniquity
Use me for what you desire me be
Look down on me I desire to toil
Sprue not me out of the race for my walk
Struggle so I won't be smoke in your nose
Great power in praying with a good heart
Within your boundaries my prayer is sweet
Heart is ready to be used for the good
For the Lion of the tribe of Judah
The God of Israel will vindicate me

II

Cannot hide from this rocky road I tread
My Lord and soul must come before my wed
Until now only sadness has been fed
Transform previous to put in my bed
By fruits of the spirit let him be led
Let him be most kind as the sword has said
Will submit to a benevolent head
Bless me because of your word I have read
I need love of the Most High God instead
Soon the damage from the words will be dead
Must two become more perfect for to wed
For my sin and others His blood was shed

I live by His holy word not just bread
Every knee shall bow as this word is spread

III

Saw them first at a young tender eighteen
Discovered world had never seen before
Submitted to change with tender kindness
Learned to fear and hate the monsters inside
Did not expect sting of the scorpion's tongue
Young mind so impressed by their charm and glare
Promised sweet tender love with passion flare
Words possess power to heal or to hurt
No slap no shove yet fierce words with mean stare
Stomach so tight when attacked and beat down
Like a knife in hands of skillful surgeon
Tiny tongue has power of life and death
Belittled confused promises broken
Was powerful pain in those words spoken

IV

Healing sprued out from the pouring rainstorm
The persecution God must now remove
Finally, she will not have to look back
They hurt her because she let them do it
The sting of the tongue can sting her no more
Yearned and desired a more kinder mate
Often wanted to lie down and take rest
Stumbled on healing power in writing
Woke up one day and felt the healing flow
That day pouring rain began to take shift
Healing power of the words from without
Words shook their sorrow then shattered their pain
Spirit brought choice words cause spirit knew them

Precious healing of mind spirit and soul

V

Open to me the windows of heaven
Let me abide under your hedges please
Rebuke the accusers for my own sake
Forgive me Lord of my transgressions too
Author and complete the faith I so need
All my sins are manifested to you
Take heed to self so you can make me new
I call on you in my time of sickness
Cast me not out but gather me to fold
Bless me according to my well doing
With all boldness I speak your Holy word
I glorify you for all you have done
I can do nothing without both of you
Jesus the father and Jesus the son

VI

Please don't tarry Lord come near unto me
I take my direction from you Most High
This is my time to wait upon you Lord
I fall on my knees and pray for your grace
I confess my sins and faults to your face
Wisdom me God in my time of sorrow
Your answers may come later or come now
Search my heart Jesus and correct me please
Cause not my mind to depart from your law
Let my healing flow from errors you saw
Let me do nothing through my vainglory
Let me do nothing through my hate or strife
I will not ask amiss from my own lusts
My ways acknowledge you and show my trust

VII

Jesus, I pray that you help me to stay
Meek humble merciful and pure in heart
Help me walk more perfect than yesterday
My desire is to follow your cue
You and only you will I seek to serve
I love you with all my heart soul and might
Remove pride from my heart so I can't fall
Make me whole so my members won't perish
Hold my tongue back from speaking ill of all
It becometh me to fulfill this quest
To live amongst your saints who are most true
Made perfect through your law this love is best
My faith remains intact trust remains stout
Am living by every word that proceed out

9

A Touch of Home

Through the phone wires, his voice stung as Aviel proudly proclaimed, *"that's how I met my wife."*

"Why is he talking to me about 'his wife'? I should have been the one he married! "What's wrong with me?" she wondered. *"Why can't the men I love, love me in return? I deserve to be treated well; don't I? If not Aviel or my ex-husband, why can't I find someone to treat me like a queen? All I want is to love and be loved. Why doesn't any man think I am pretty enough? Why doesn't any man think I am smart enough? Why doesn't any man think I am worthy enough to be an adored wife?"*

Maayan knew her sister saw Aviel the other day and gave him her number. She expected this phone call from her old flame, but this was not what she anticipated.

"Shalom Aleichem achoti, pretty lady. I heard about your divorce, is it finalized yet? I'm here if you need me," Aviel offered.

It was nice to know he was concerned even if he had ulterior motives, *"A lot has happened since I last saw you. How is life?"* she responded, in an attempt to change the subject.

"Life is good. I've missed you! I've grown a lot since we broke up."

Aviel was always frank about his feelings. He was a lady's man, and it was ultimately the reason their relationship ended. That was one thing for sure Maayan knew she couldn't deal with. He was into multiplying his love amongst beautiful women.

"I've been through trials and tribulations, and probably learned a lesson or two I wish I hadn't. Occasionally, I've thought about you as well. So, it's nice to hear your voice," she admitted.

But the truth was, she thought about him often, and even more so when her ex-husband was emotionally negligent.

"I heard through the grapevine you haven't been smiling much. You should let me change that. I always loved your smile," he added.

Maayan heard through the grapevine Aviel was single again. So, she was taken aback when he professed his love for his new wife. Her stomach twisted in knots, knowing he has married yet again. With her marriage dissolved, she had hoped for an opportunity to be the object of his affection again.

"Maybe this time you'll be a better husband." She didn't really mean it, but it was the right thing to say. *"Which one is this? Your third? Right?"* she stabbed, trying to ignore her own pain. *"Are you*

still in Texas? I heard you moved there with your second wife," Maayan added, twisting the knife a little deeper.

Her ears picked up his light snickering through the phone. Aviel was used to these kinds of passive-aggressive attacks. He faced it often from the women who found themselves tangled in his web of love.

"You know I can't be still for too long," Aviel joked. *"Adivah, my second wife couldn't deal with it either."*

Maayan knew exactly what that meant. Aviel had a gentle and kind approach, but his heart would always be divided.

"Do you remember Yaffa? She and I came to Chi-Town together for the summer."

Maayan interrupted *"Yes, I remember Yaffa, the woman who is not your wife?"* Stab!

Aviel sucked his teeth as if almost annoyed. *"Yes, Yaffa, the woman who is not my wife."* He continued. *"She came along to keep me company as I attended to some family business. But we will be heading back to Texas soon. You know I have to make that money in order to keep up with all my hunnys,"* he stabbed back. *"That's beside the point though. I can hardly wait to see you again in a beautiful summer dress. You know how I love a pretty lady sashaying around in a sundress!*" he added trying to make love and not war.

"Is that supposed to be a compliment?" she asked sarcastically, trying to hide the fact she secretly enjoyed any and every compliment he gave her no matter how double handed it was.

"Yes, and I have more waiting for you if you play nice. I must admit it took me a minute to find your phone number; I misplaced it amongst my other numbers."

"Well, I see you found it."

"You know how persistent I am when I want something. Can I take you to lunch before I leave?"

She knew exactly what he meant. It seems she and Adivah walked away from Aviel for the same reason. Maayan began to notice this toxic cycle of them entertaining the same conversations as they dipped and dabbed in and out of each other's lives. She naively held on hoping Aviel would change. She hoped he would be more settled and loyal. And more than anything she hoped he was single.

"You know I will always love you; you will always be my first love," he swooned.

"You always have a warm place in my heart too Avee. But you know I am not the type of woman to infiltrate another sister's space," she proclaimed,

feeling slightly unsure of whether she was trying to convince herself or him.

She never envisioned after their last encounter eleven years ago that he'd be married, again! This was not a reality she welcomed. There was an ache in the pit of her stomach, the place where emotions lounge. Aviel always found her; she got a random call from him every so often. These were calls she welcomed, no matter how unfruitful.

Like most young girls, Maayan wanted to be a loving and devoted wife. Often in her marriage, her heart would ache from not being touched by a warm and kind man. She often felt herself withering away because of her husband's constant detachment. She remembered feeling abandoned and rejected. This wasn't a feeling with which she could grow to be accustomed. A wife is supposed to be comforted and protected by her husband.

Over the years, she realized no matter the age, a woman perpetually loves when she is loved deeply. She felt imprisoned by the lack of companionship from her husband. The irony was she never wanted to be alone, yet she always felt alone even when he was laying in the bed next to her. She longed to be a loving and respectful wife. She earnestly desired to reap the love she diligently sowed.

Not a day went by when she didn't daydream about being a wife to a loving husband. Not a week went by when she didn't think about how she should respond to the kindness of a loving husband. Not a month went by when a tear did not fall from the wells of her eyes as her thoughts tried to bloom through the rocky soil her marriage was built upon.

Her passion drove her, like one of Langston Hughes' dreams deferred, a fantasy that would not be fulfilled.

She remembered the first time she laid eyes on Aviel years ago, in the South Shore High School auditorium. It was the last assembly, before winter break. He stood there, smiling at her from not far away. Maayan remembered how she caught his eye; she returned the smile and he received it as a welcome message. She could feel his smile permeate her; it reached in and touched her soul.

His smile was a warm, comfortable and tender touch; it marked her heart for life. It would never leave her because she didn't want to ever let it go. She felt at home with him. Her feet would not move; they were steadfast. They felt heavy and light at the same time. She did not want her legs to carry her away. His eyes set her heart ablaze. They reached her soul. She was helpless with no defense from his allure.

In the beginning, she was excited to feel him feeling her. She always felt vulnerable because, at the age of sixteen, Maayan's father was supposed to show her the love she sought from others. She needed the comfort of a strong man in her life. She needed the encouragement of a loving father to guide her and make her feel pretty. It was a critical thing; it could have protected her from the smile Aviel radiated her way that unforgettable day.

Though Maayan did have a father, he wasn't willing to be colored a real dad. He was not engaged in her life, which left her open and vulnerable. She needed love, and it seemed she was falling in love right there, in the auditorium, with this fine young man and his warm smile. Aviel's smile was not seductive. It invited her and made her trust him. He momentarily locked her into his grasp. It was only natural for her to respond with an unquestionable and an enthusiastic *"Yes!"* when Aviel asked, *"Will you give me a chance to love you?"*

She doesn't remember what happened to that comfort she interpreted at their first encounter. She couldn't remember where it went wrong when it went sour. In real life, love at first sight, is most often a recipe for disaster. Aviel and Maayan's story was no different. Maayan thought it would be one of those happily ever after stories like Cinderella. In the story, Prince Charming was a love possessed man searching high and low, day and night for the mysterious beauty with which he danced at the ball. Unbeknownst to him, his true love was squandering away as a mere servant girl. As the story is told, the day Cinderella's foot was made a match to the slipper was her moment of reckoning. But do we know what really happened? Did she really live happily ever after?

As Maayan thought back, she knew she should have been more cautious. Even after so many years, his eyes, his voice, and his touch burned intensely. She was defenseless as if in a crossfire. She remembered how disillusioned she was before as she tried to reconnect with his comforting smile and that initial spirit of trust that overtook her in the high school auditorium. That was what she longed for all these years. This is what she could never forget. This is what she could not stop feeling. This is what haunted her in her flawed marriage. This is what continued to haunt her now as she approached this new phase of her life.

As she stood in the auditorium, frozen and unable to move or speak, she never thought she'd be his star-crossed lover, destined to be a part of him, as he loved someone else over and over again. She remembered making love to him that laudable first time and then that wretched last time. She basked in the glory of feeling the arms of her lover again, when he stopped in mid-stroke to ask her, *"Who have you been sleeping with?"*

At that moment she forgot to enjoy his touch, to enjoy his smell, to enjoy being in his arms again. She began to grieve before the act was complete. She mourned as he walked her home. *"I'll never stop trying,"* she said to herself as she climbed those five stairs and he backed away from her reach. What caused this unsavory stench? Those words, *"I'll never stop trying,"* imbued her brain, they sketched a permanent scar across her heart. It was a mark that would haunt her for many years.

Part of her scarred heart would always belong to Aviel. It would always long for him. Like a drug, it would still yearn for that introductory sensation. That sensation that flowed through her and spread like the wings of a butterfly. She felt all this upon their first glance in the high school auditorium. Those feelings of comfort, trust, protection and love, would never leave her. Her memories would not go away. Instead, over time, they intensified and willed him in and out of her life. They haunted her with the uncertainty of what could have been, what she wished it were. What she feared it would never be. She could have been content there if he could commit his love solely to her.

Before their conversation on the phone ended, he offered to make her part of his life. He said he'd do it her way. He offered to keep it private, just between the two of them. But Maayan couldn't be anybody's secret life. So instead, he proposed to include her into his life slowly. He was confident he could get his wife to agree. But Maayan could not be responsible for breaking another sister's heart; becoming a sister wife was not her cup of tea. She wanted neither his pity, nor to be his pawn. Yet, she wanted him to hear her laugh so he wouldn't know how sad she really was. It was one of the most tragic and loneliest smiles she'd ever felt before. In an attempt to escape from his poisonous love, she concocted a story which required this unhealthy exchange to come to an end.

"Avee, it's been good talking to you, but I have to get off the phone."

"Hey, babe don't be like that. It's nothing but love. If you allow me, I can love you like no other. You know I'm the only one that can love you right!"

"Yea… It's been real, but I gotta go." She quickly said, *"Goodbye, Avee,"* and hung up before he could convince her otherwise.

After she hung up the receiver, she knew she had to hang up every desire and illicit thought she ever had about Aviel. She began to think about the man with whom she embarked on a marriage with. Where she lived in loneliness. She never understood why she was married and felt so alone. That marriage did not feel like home. She realized in her ignorance how her adulterous thoughts for Aviel began to deteriorate her marriage before it even started. She considered her husband a shack leaving her wanton for shelter and Aviel was the only shelter she desired.

Her thoughts caused her to feel somber, as tears ran down her face. *"Who will love me now? What's wrong with me? Did my hands help play the fiddle that led to its end and demise?"* The Dells song, *"The Love We Had Stays on My Mind"* played over and over again as she lay there thinking of Aviel and how she would never get a chance to be loved by him, to be touched by him, or to have him repossess her youth now gone and forgotten.

In each moment, she listened to the song and she felt more hopeless to this "dream deferred." She felt a surge of anger rise from the place where she stored her longing. She was not his helpmeet. He didn't choose her. She was not the one chosen to encourage him. She didn't get the joy of supporting his dreams. She was not his companion. It was not her pleasure to be his inspiration. She was not commissioned to help make him feel good about himself. She was not his mate.

Her obscure emotions constantly left her open and vulnerable. She had her moment of reckoning, when she realized she willed the keys to her freedom and all she had to do was simply move on. Maybe if she stopped hunting a ghost, she could have invested more energy in finding new love or making her marriage work.

Her toxic thoughts started again, *"How could he not know? How could he not feel me? Maybe he does know, but he clearly doesn't care?"* she considered. *"How can I learn to stop being in love with a dream?"* She tried to muster up at least a soft smile for Aviel's happy life. She wondered how many times love could break the same heart. This would be the last time Maayan would accept one of these calls.

Maayan stopped the thoughts before they grew from anger to ugliness, which lies inside of bitterness. She needed to unearth the touch of home within herself. She was suddenly relieved at her fresh thoughts and felt renewed because, in the stillness of her mind, she quickly and silently called upon her Creator for help. *"Keep back thy servant also from presumptuous sins; let them not have dominion over me,"* she recalled the scripture prayed:

Father help my self-image.
Help me to find identity in you
understand my worth
value your standards
recognize my unique qualities designed by you
Lord, to you I pray

Help me to appreciate me
see myself the way you see me
understand that you Lord fashioned me too a
    little lower than the angels
view you as my author and designer
Lord, before you these things I lay

Help me to see you crowned me with glory and honor
to know you made me to have dominion over the
    creation as well
understand you put all things under my feet to boot
ask you to quiet the voice that whispers otherwise
seek your satisfaction and yours alone
Lord, I utter your praise today

Help me to hear your voice
taste your perfection
realize you will make my life successful
comprehend I have no power perceive real
realize all power is yours,
Father, give me ears to say

"Have mercy upon me, O God, according to thy
loving-kindness: according unto the multitude of
thy tender mercies blot out my transgressions.
Wash me throughly from mine iniquity, and
cleanse me from my sin. For I acknowledge my
transgressions: and my sin is ever before me.
Against thee, thee only, have I sinned, and done
this evil in thy sight: that thou mightest be
justified when thou speakest, and be clear when
thou judgest."

In that instance she learned she needed to love herself; find comfort and solace in the one who created her. At that moment she knew her happiness was not tied to the love of any man. She realized her happiness was tied to The Most High and at last she was done.

10

Fragrance of Love

My husband is the father of many nations as prophesied. Yah showed me in a dream he would be revered among Israelites, Edomites, Muslims, and Christians worldwide for generations to come. In this dream, I saw he would be the progenitor of Shem, the father of all Semitic people and cultures. He was a faithful man whom I respected long before I fell in love with him. I bore my husband six sons. My respect for him grew every day as I witnessed him show kindness to others around us.

I have nothing but honor and admiration for Sarah as well. As her handmaiden, I knew her well; she was my longtime friend, and I was her confidant. Sarah taught me how to pray; this was one of the greatest gifts she imparted to me. I comforted her in her last days and attended to her every need. Because I was a constant presence in their lives, people began to speculate I had become Abraham's concubine while Sarah was alive. But, because of my admiration for her, I won't attest whether or not I ever touched her husband and he ever touched me while Sarah was still alive.

Abraham and I fell in love after he saw how tenderly I cared for Sarah. After she saw our connection develop, she gave us her blessings. Sarah loved Abraham with all her heart. Not wanting him to be alone or feel guilty; she facilitated a relationship between us, which eventually blossomed.

I watched how Hagar, the Egyptian handmaiden, and Ishmael, her son, disrespected Sarah and her son Isaac. I knew that was a grave mistake. Though God blessed her womb, Hagar didn't grow in the fruit of the spirit. Instead, she became insolent. After she got pregnant, Hagar segregated herself from the sisterhood Sarah worked so hard to build. Whether Hagar's pride in her pregnancy was subtle or overt, Sarah picked up on it immediately, and she didn't like it. Hagar thought she was better than everyone else. Here this woman invites you into her home to bear children for such a faithful man as Abraham, with no regard for herself or her feelings, and you show your true colors? Humph!

Hagar's illicit behavior continued after Ishmael was born. She refused to teach him how to love and respect his brother. This was part of her downfall. God established Sarah as Abraham's first wife; she was the one whom He chose to carry the seed who would inherit the birthright. Hagar failed to understand that! Even if Isaac was chosen to carry the birthright, it did not mean God was not omnipotent enough to ensure all our sons would be blessed. I tried to remind Hagar, but she didn't listen. Obviously, she wasn't the sharpest tool, nor the wisest of women. She had the audacity to despise Sarah and look at her with contempt just because Sarah could not bear Abraham a child.

Hagar provoked Sarah until she could bear no more. Sarah told Abraham to rid us of Hagar's wickedness. Hagar must have forgotten she was only the surrogate. She did not remember Sarah chose her, not Abraham. My heart was broken that day; I was hoping it would never come to that point.

Had Hagar considered, she could have contemplated that God would not object to her being expelled from the camp. Regardless of the nation from which we came, as members of Abraham's household, we were mandated to serve The Most High. We were all obligated to learn more about the eternal Elohim every day. It became natural for us to pray and build our trust in Him. Yet and still, Hagar had to learn the hard way.

I remember how livid Abraham was, as he reminded Hagar constantly to circumcise Ishmael; she knew that was a rule of the house. Her slothful attitude almost cost Ishmael his life. If it weren't for Abraham's steadfastness, Hagar would have broken the covenant, which is why Abraham circumcised Ishmael himself at the age of thirteen. Hagar was one disobedient woman. I don't know why she thought Abraham would love her more than he loved Sarah or God's commandments. I tried to warn her, but the poor thing was just confused.

As Sarah and Hagar's relationship continued to disintegrate; it became apparent to everyone Abraham wanted nothing to do with the whole situation. He only conceded in the first place because Sarah insisted. In her lack of faith, Sarah couldn't see the promise to come; the only way she fathomed "obtaining children" was by her Egyptian servant girl. As things continued to spiral out of control, Sarah confided in me. Choosing Hagar was a mistake; she only wanted to fulfill God's promise.

One day, Sarah watched Ishmael taunt Isaac while Hagar candidly sat by watching. That was the straw that broke the camel's back. We were stunned when Sarah laid hands on Hagar. My mouth hung open. I knew Sarah; she was humble, kind, and meek, but that day all fruit of the spirit flew out the window. Sarah slapped Hagar senseless.

The other handmaidens and I tried to warn Hagar; she was getting too arrogant and headed down the wrong path. Still, she wouldn't listen. Sarah was not a jealous woman; but Hagar provoked her constantly. We all thought Hagar's behavior was deleterious. There was nothing Godly about it. Sarah tried to be patient before she made Abraham put her out. It didn't take long for Hagar to learn her place and see the error in her ways.

You could say I learned from Hagar too. I learned what not to do if I didn't want Sarah to lay hands on me. Hagar's expulsion was the talk of the camp, and some people thought Abraham was being unjust when he put the girl out with not enough rations for her journey. Abraham was certainly caught in the middle of a situation. What was he supposed to do? He didn't want to know what was going on with the women, so he did nothing—like most men.

Abraham didn't want to deal with it, he gave Hagar no added attention and no extra energy. He never tried to force Hagar into submission, and he let her hang herself. Why should he have to inflict pain upon her anyway? She did the job his wife asked her to do; she got pregnant. Her job was done, Hagar was Sarah's handmaid, so he let her handle it. But that wasn't enough for Sarah, because Hagar kept provoking her, he was too passive about the entire situation, so Sarah told him what to do, what she thought was best!

You can't make this stuff up. But, in hindsight, maybe had Abraham been more proactive, this entire situation may never have transpired. His inactivity was the reason Hagar felt comfortable mocking Sarah. You should have seen Hagar's smirk drop when Abraham quieted his wife's rage. In the beginning Abraham was reluctant, until the Most High stepped in. I was the one who heard

Sarah's prayers every morning as I tended to her needs. I heard her praying for the best on behalf of her family, including Hagar.

When Hagar returned from expulsion, she was a changed woman. We could tell she learned to listen to the voice of The Most High. She elaborated to me how difficult it was for her in the desert. First of all, why in the heck did she walk towards the desert anyway, especially knowing she had limited rations? She should have walked in the opposite direction, where she would have found vegetation and water. That showed me how many screws were really loose in Hagar's head. It would have taken longer, but the land would have provided for her until she got to Egypt. Her saving grace was Ishmael. The Most High heard the lad's cry and put his hedges of protection around them, keeping them safe until they returned to us.

God sometimes calls us to account for our inappropriate behavior in our wanderings from His perfect will. Hagar's time in the desert was her opportunity to fully understand the faith Abraham and Sarah tried to impart to her. In the end, it all worked out. Sarah forgave Hagar; she did not mistreat her, but she would not trust her again. Hagar remained in the shadows after that. I felt sorry for her.

In her later days, I grew closer to Sarah and served her well. I learned everything I could from her. She was a virtuous woman; up early looking well to the needs of her household and teaching us to be submissive and cunning in prayer. Sarah died with no daughters, but she had many handmaidens. Every day she gathered us for prayer and worship.

On the Shabbat eve she invited us into her tent for bread and wine. Those were good times, and we had so much fun. We talked about everything and laughed a lot. She encouraged sisterhood, and she taught us to love each other as we learned the ways of Abraham's God and built our faith in Him. Every night she prayed for each of us. I listened to her pray for her husband and her son at least three times every day until the day she gave up the ghost.

Once Sarah died, Abraham commissioned a team of men servants to escort Hagar and Ishmael to her homeland, where she would be happier. By then, Hagar understood her son would become many nations too as The Most High promised Abraham. In Egypt, Ishmael took a wife and started his own family having twelve sons. As a promise to Sarah, Abraham vowed Isaac would live in peace as the only son. Which meant when his other sons came of age, Abraham sent them away, but he did not let them leave empty-handed; he sent them away with a substantial inheritance. He wanted them to be men of wealth and standards. He wanted them esteemed in the lands where they decided to dwell.

11

Winds of Rose

I

This sequestered year brought with it knew light
She felt winded unnerved lonely today
People she thought she knew gave her new sight
God used "Friends" as source of new things to say
Her eyes view pity, rather than just hurt
There is a heartfelt sad deep within she
Sister Care Too Much tries always to flirt
Sister Called Hurt came by the house lately
Sister Self Pity is a willing host
Suddenly the fourth one knocks at her door
Sister Anger sneaks in long and gets close
A viral and vigorous team of four
She claims these four sisters, "they're surely mine"
Permeated sister winds over time.

II

A new sister peeped through door around ten
She vaguely recalls her spying you see
She is different from those other women
Gaining strength defines her menially
She's more like the strong aroma of myrrh
She saw other sisters sneak out the back
Sister Overcome more likely names her
They talked for a while, she's sharp as a tack

She however sees clearly who she is
Eyes shined with a clear determination
The Gospel of peace oozed out from the source,
Her feet were shod with the preparation
Couldn't have been just an overnight thing
She could hear her sing praises to the king.

III

Today was their first long talk, they would cry
Circumstances cause lives to look the same
Who is like God is the name she goes by;
Disposition more than a simple name
Polished, shined, tested, tried and now refined
Almost gave in when trials went bad to worse
Lately though her faith prayer was defined
Sister cried out when life seemed a bad curse
Mirrors the same, wouldn't give up the fight
Couldn't tell from her smile but she'd seen hell
They compared scars, talked battle up til night
She's The Purple Rose, just Rose for this tale
Fight was not hers, so she refused to fall
Said she'd seen too much to tell it all.

IV

The tale of Rose is not from fresh new fruit
Rose was not prepared for the tears she wept
Winds of life blows on us all, same ol root
Her first wind left Rose feeling low and swept
She recalls praying for a man who knew

She thought she could love enough to withstand
If God is love, then she ignored the cue
She didn't know she was afoot hot sand
Fugitived and charred was Rose's young life
Eschewed patience, she rushed in way too soon
All she wanted: to be a loving wife
The Scorpion made Rose sing a new tune
A winded tune she'd learn to sing too well
Pierced heart, ripped, cowed, it was hopeless to tell.

V

Their first conversation went much like this
"I am a passionate man and so then,
I need a passionate woman." Sealed kiss.
What he really meant. "My emotions send
me in a rage because of jealous eyes."
Beat down by his tongue made a useless pulp
Maya Angelou's words rang: "Still I Rise"
Rose could not rise, pill too big to gulp
No healing rang from the reviling tongue
It lashed, it hurt, it pierced, cut Rose deep
It stenched of pure dung and skillfully sung
She aversely sat in his darkened creep
Terrorized and crushed and all the time
Who could Rose tell of this heinous crime?

VI

Sold Rose the dream while her eyes were still fixed
Calumnied, maligned, abated, shamed

Rose felt like it was her mind playing tricks
Sang hatred and anger with eyes inflamed
Sang praises at sometimes so proud and great
Bewildered, perplexed, confusing as heck
Up and down, off and on, love and hate; wait
Rose pondered trying to ring her own neck
Trained to doubt her own sanity and mind
Set up, crippled, yearning for what's less hot
Accused then praised, cussed out then spoke to kind
Sometimes in front of others sometimes not
Not certain whether she should smile or cry
Thinking about a way to say goodbye.

VII

Not barefoot she was pregnant as always
Incapacitated by her nurture.
Tried to do the right thing bearing his ways:
Criticized lame, crushed; and freedom searched her.
Fell to the floor to cry out to God, please
She cried for many years with a sad face
Her recourse was simply, drop to torn knees
Disregarded wedded wife was her place
She glimpsed "Rose" from the mirror on the wall
Hidden behind the aging, frowned, sad she
She heard a faint distressing inner call
Look, wake up, and open your eyes, it's me
Gather your little ones, now, they need hope
Otherwise, they will never learn to cope.

VIII

Startled and shaken by light she could see
She vaguely recalled the years that slipped by
Gone was her sunshine, yet she chose to flee
When her first-borns moaned, wept, and when they cried
Finally, opening her tear stained eyes
Each had scars in dire need of mending
Rose could now hear her children's private cries
Waiting for her to see to their tending
The beatings her son received must now end
Her daughter's beatdowns must come to a halt
She knew well his pride wouldn't let him bend
Watching, children will be what they are taught
She had to make a clear choice for her lot
It was time to leap from the seething pot.

IX

She pleaded to God like never before
Afraid of God's eternal burning flame
While making plans to let butt hit the door
Transforming strength now burned within her frame.
We have all fallen short of God's glory
Who can stand in time of His great coming?
Rose can testify of her grim story
Amid fear, relief, freedom succumbing.
She had no idea what she would now do
Though she knew to keep her eyes rooted up
No mercy though worship family knew

Prayed for strength to carry this bitter cup
Shaky and scared, she gathered strength to pack
Teared Rose did not want to ever go back.

X

Rose didn't want to go back to devil's spell
"You are trifling, I don't want you now?"
 "You are stupid," Rose dared go against hell
"You are a whore," "Whose baby is it now?"
"You have no virtue," he would yell and yell
"You are a good wife," then "why did I vow?"
 "You are my love," then "foolish slut," Rose fell
Hit bang slam bleeding heart hurt bend and bow
"Please don't send me back to revile and rail"
"Oh God please how much more will you allow?"
Why was she alone lonely in a jail?
How could she break this wrong and ugly vow?
Caress or curse fond loath love or hate rap?
Rejected or protected kiss or slap?

XI

Rose had no warning what more could have come
No one could have paid her a million bucks
Stony hearted him made her heart beat numb
Ignoring his seed evidenced pure nuts
His rejection heightened their acute scars
Here lies a Bible teaching infidel
Worse thing she had seen in this curse by far

But she too was a sinner who could fail
Reflecting back on what has now gone past
On his sin, she should not have fixed her eyes
Serpent lurched a trick he leeched on her fast
Tumultuous wind: near loss of the prize
Lil Big Man, tempest winds for short while
Fabricated a lie that stole her smile.

XII

Contrived, simulation of a best friend
Skillful deception and again Rose cried
From pillow to pillow, floor to floor, and den to den
She contemplated doom because he lied
She was not supposed to be his secret
Rejection sourced all of her inbred fears
He tried to alter that for which she was meant
Cut as deep as the first winds years of tears
Naiveté was an enemy to Rose
Imagine if you dare, your heart ripped out
This describes pain that would curl up her toes
Acute, severe suffering, darkened doubt
Jesus stepped in before her breath took flight
Sent prayer, praise, Bible, pen, and his might.

XIII

What happened to her Sisters in Prayer?
Cunning women of prayer were not there
The winds abandoned her as she stood frayed

Deliverance vow broken as they stare
Repulsion and abandonment held fast
Shadowed pain bitterly through day and night
Left alone to taste torment hardly cast
She was tossed, wound up and bound very tight
But it was the fault of this tainted Rose
Since Jesus gave already instructions
Bitterness hovered her heart that slammed close
God said, "trust no man", nor their seductions
Man is both male and friend fickle female
Rose quenched a shout, "All 'yall go straight to hell!

XIV

Nevertheless, words for Rose wisped trust God
Bid care to male or female so freely
Refrain fluent voice bench tranquilly nod
Heart and mind belong to no one but He
Word taught to forgive for forgiveness sake
She had nothing to hold against others
She wanted no part of the hot filled lake
Wished well to all the sisters and brothers
Alone yet full with hope, she can now live
Mending the tears in her heart which she bare
Not everyone knows how to love nor give
Neither angry nor bitter; Rose can't care
Erasing the shadowy tears of fear
Refined, awaiting her time and her year.

XV

This almost ends her saga for just now
Empowered by a makeover of mind
More winds might blow her way as Rose learns how
To let lose tainted dreams poorly designed
Each frustration brings a different sort
Of challenge rage tragedy utter loss
Preparation for judgement at last court
Some speak of boll weevils, rain, draught, or moss
All touched by beauty and some classed by fame
Some speak in sonnet, ballad, or free verse
All will have to bow to God's mighty name
Life is given to practice and rehearse
Rose is no exception to this great plan
Same question; "Who shall be able to stand?"

XVI

Sister Care Too Much has since gone and split
Sister Called Hurt left just the other day
Rose had no mind to really notice it
Sister Anger was not the last to stay
Sister Self Pity grieved Lil Big Man
Inhaled deeply she tried hard to let go
He was supposed to ask her for her hand
Bruised gash lingered dense til Rose avowed, "NO!"
Rose solely thought of the Scorpion when
Matters of the children came to her mind
His seed she will forever have to tend

Otherwise he is pushed back far behind
Rose and she are one, we talk the same talk
She is Rose's mirror; Rose is her walk.

XVII

Emotional abstinence, pleasant calm
Uncomplaining of circumstances bound
Cool. Using the Word as her soothing balm
Quiet. Not uttering a single sound
Temperately bearing the inertia
Repress the pain of annoying hardship
Indifferent to life's militia
Consciously letting God steer the big ship
Song of hope long: walking through the twelve gates
Song of joy dance: giving Him constant praise
Song of peace be still: she quietly waits
Song of virtue strong: through tumult and maze
Fruited from The Purple Rose: meet patience,
Having her perfect work, experience.

www.ingramcontent.com/pod-product-compliance
Lightning Source LLC
Chambersburg PA
CBHW020659180626
46816CB00003B/1368